LOU SKELTON

Send Me One Back?

eight eclectic stories of gay erotic romance

First published by Lou Skelton 2021

Cover design by Lou Skelton

First edition

ISBN: 978-1-7397861-1-3

This book was professionally typeset on Reedsy.
Find out more at reedsy.com

Many thanks to all the people who have believed in me over the past few years. You never know what a kind word and a bit of enthusiasm can do for others—in my case, it led to what I hope will be the first of many books.

Contents

Reader advisory and notes on content

Readers should be advised that this book contains sexually explicit content and is not suitable for those under 18. The stories vary in topic and theme but all feature consenting adults. Most contain graphic sex scenes and a few contain several.

Included below are a few notes on the content of each story and which may contain spoilers. A list of content warnings is also available on my website at louskelton.com/content.

- *The End of the Line:* voyeurism, sex in public, sex with a stranger
- *Satori:* depression, mentions of grief and bereavement
- *Of Camaraderie and Corruption:* apparent dubious consent, apparent coercion, master/servant relationship, minor humiliation, corruption of an innocent trope, themes of domination and revenge
- *Inside Looking Out:* set during the coronavirus pandemic, voyeurism
- *The Price of Admission:* supernatural elements, voyeurism, dubious consent, memory loss
- *Meeting Isaac:* character engaged in sex work, anxiety, self-esteem issues, some discussion around shame and especially in relation to sex
- *Devotions:* set in a fictional religious order where sex is part of worship, themes of chastity, D/s dynamics

- *Send Me One Back:* mention of non-consensual photo sharing

1

The End of the Line

Charlie took the escalator at a trot, his messenger bag banging against his hip as he descended into the hot, dry air of the tube station. From below floated the vibrating squall of a train. The sound rose with the growing breeze, whipping open his jacket and rearranging his hair. He ran down the last few steps and hurried onto the platform. The wind there was strong, blowing at his back as he dodged around those already waiting at the safety doors. The train screeched and slowed; he made it to the end of the platform with seconds to spare. The doors slid open. A few people got out; the few who'd arrived before him got on. Charlie hopped aboard and there it was, the holy grail: one seat left at the end of the carriage. Perfect.

The doors beeped shut as he claimed it, exhilarated with his success. A seat meant more than mere comfort. A seat meant he had seventeen minutes of peace in which to add to a design proposal and to catch up on a few emails. Charlie unzipped his laptop from its case and balanced it in his lap. His headphones were wrapped around his neck, waiting. He slipped them on and music filled his ears, not quite drowning out the screech of the speeding train.

It swerved in a familiar rhythm beneath him; bumping, rocking, slowing, then accelerating again. The sensation would have been soothing if not for the growing crush inside the carriage. People were now edging carefully down the aisle. Bags swung past him as they were taken down from their owners' shoulders; someone trod on his foot. Charlie kept his head down and concentrated on his screen.

Stations passed: Canary Wharf, Canada Water, Bermondsey. At London Bridge, a number of people filed off and the person opposite nearly missed his stop. He swept his bags up in a rush and forced his way through those already boarding the train. The wave of incoming passengers paused to let him pass and then resumed. New faces swelled into the carriage, occupying coveted nooks by the doors or taking smug possession of freshly-emptied seats. As they found their places and stilled, the train began to move once again.

But it was a false start. The train jerked violently and halted, causing its lights to flicker and all the passengers to stumble. A couple of those standing made a grab for the overhead bars; Charlie's shoulder collided with the woman sitting next to him. He slid his headphones off one ear to apologise and heard the driver's weary voice sighing through the intercom. *Please do not lean on the doors.* When the train finally left the station, its sharp acceleration left all the passengers bracing themselves to stay upright.

A calm descended; everyone went back to their inner thoughts and their phones. Charlie turned up the volume of his music. But before he could absorb himself in his work, he became aware that he was being watched.

The sensation was unmistakable: a prickling, uncanny shiver which made Charlie instinctively look up. Sitting not-quite-opposite was a man. A paper was lying ignored in his lap and he was staring out of the tunnel-dark window just next to Charlie's ear. A beat passed. The man, jolted by a particularly abrupt motion of the train, came back to himself. Oblivious to Charlie's frown, he turned his attention smoothly back to his paper.

Weird, thought Charlie as he focused again on his emails. But, he reminded himself, jarring moments like that were common on the tube. With so many people packed into one small space, it was easy to accidentally intrude into someone else's consciousness. The man, no doubt, had meant nothing by it.

And yet Charlie's attention kept wandering from his work. He couldn't escape a nagging feeling that it had been more than an accident, and he glanced up at the man for a second time.

He had a subtly compelling appearance, Charlie decided. At first sight, he seemed older than he really was but, confusingly, a second might cause an observer to think the opposite. His dress was the reason: pin-sharp, tailored, immaculate; classic in an old-fashioned way. He wore a serious-looking tie of just the right width, fastened with a pin, and his shirt was gleaming and bright. There was a monogrammed briefcase tucked behind his ankles and he had a pair of leather gloves cradled in his lap. His face, partly hidden behind the newspaper, revealed he was a man in his early forties. And the details of his suit—cut, fabric, a silver flash of cufflinks—suggested he was the real article. Real tailoring, real money.

Politics or banking? Charlie wondered. He returned to his emails, scrolling through their subject lines. Or was he something else, something more unusual—fine arts dealer? Antiques? An unspecified 'creative' on his way to a meeting? He considered these options idly, deleting emails and drafting others. By the time they arrived at his stop, the mystery man was nowhere to be seen. Charlie packed his things away and forgot him as soon as he'd left the train.

But that evening, on his way home, the man was there again, sitting in almost exactly the same seat. Charlie hadn't noticed his arrival. He'd looked up after Westminster and there he was, looking as crisp and unruffled as he had that morning.

Politics or banking, Charlie asked himself again. How much easier it would be if he could lean over and say *excuse me, hope you don't mind me asking, but do you happen to work in finance?*

The man had arranged himself as comfortably as it was possible to be on the tube. His briefcase was wedged into place on the floor behind his calves, his gloves were in his lap, and there was a half-folded *Evening Standard* in front of his face. Charlie studied him from the corner of his eye. His movements were precise; particular but not fussy. He turned a page of the paper with a soft snap, glanced at it briefly, then turned the page again. One hand played absently with the gloves resting across his thighs. His fingers were well-formed; long and fine-boned, but not thin. As London Bridge approached, he folded away the newspaper and pulled the gloves on. He flexed his fingers once to ensure a correct fit; black leather stretched elegantly across his knuckles. The gloves were snug, lightweight—expensive and possibly handmade? As the train stopped, the man tucked the paper under his arm, picked up his briefcase, and departed. Charlie watched until his dark, upright figure disappeared into the crowd.

Over the next few weeks, the man with the briefcase became

a regular fixture of Charlie's journeys. Sometimes one of them had to sit or stand in another part of the carriage, and sometimes the man wasn't on the same train at all. But he was there often enough for Charlie to learn his habits.

He travelled only between London Bridge and Green Park. Apart from the briefcase, he carried with him a newspaper and occasionally an umbrella. His suits were always dark and beautifully pressed, worn with a tailored wool overcoat (unbuttoned) and a woven silk scarf. Sometimes he wore a hat, but mostly he went bareheaded: his hair was thick, dark and sleek, and parted at the side. The gloves were a constant. On every journey, he would take a seat, remove them with care, and then keep them in his lap while he read his newspaper. It was hard for Charlie to study his face without making his curiosity obvious. From what he'd seen it was nice but not remarkable; clean-shaven, with good clear skin. His expressions were minimal as, like all tube passengers, he operated at a careful neutral. Charlie guessed that he would be considered good-looking once away from the unflattering fluorescent lights and tired yawns of the Underground.

Once, when out to buy a lunchtime sandwich, Charlie saw ahead of him the tall silhouette of a man in a well-cut coat. He also thought he'd glimpsed the swing of a briefcase, and a gloved hand around its handle, but couldn't be sure if his mind had added that afterwards. Had it been him? Green Park was not that far from Oxford Street—but neither was it near. A division seemed to lay between the two, protected by an invisible barrier which seemed difficult to cross on foot.

But that was nonsense, Charlie told himself as he pushed through the shopping throng. There were any number of reasons it could have been him: a meeting, an errand, a passing fancy. Anyone could be stumbled across on Oxford Street, so why not the man on the train?

He returned back to his desk and checked his calendar. He had a call with a new client at four and nothing much to distract himself with until then. The sandwich he'd bought was dry and disappointing, despite—or perhaps because of—its claims to health and nutrition. He ate without giving it much attention and then opened a new suite of tabs in preparation for the afternoon's work.

It doesn't really matter if it was him or not, Charlie thought. He's just a man on the tube, nothing to do with me. He's Green Park and I'm Oxford Street. That's all.

One Friday afternoon, during a particularly dull meeting, a picture came to him. The sun was shining outside; a triangle of blue sky glowed jewel-like between the sash window and the flat grey roof of the building opposite. Spring was creeping in, stirring the stale meeting room air with a sluggish breeze. But the image in Charlie's mind announced itself all at once. The man on the train, with his thighs spread and trousers open, his hard cock gripped by greased leather fingers. Charlie was appalled. Rajiv was just going through the figures for the past quarter and it was almost his slot on the agenda. It was the worst possible time to be having thoughts of that nature.

He made himself refocus, helped along by the fear that he'd have to use a strategically placed notebook to present his slides. But, after the meeting, the picture returned again, bigger and brighter and more finely drawn. In it, leather gleamed wet and shiny, and there were sounds as well, soft ones, and the crisp rustle of a newspaper. Concentrating became difficult. Charlie frowned at himself, annoyed at his misfiring brain and its bad sense of timing.

He left work early, complaining of a headache. He had hoped to avoid further encouraging his imagination by missing that evening's encounter with the man on the train. But it didn't work, and somehow the man boarded at Green Park as usual.

In vain, Charlie tried to keep his eyes on his laptop—but then there came the familiar movements and he could not prevent himself from watching. The gloves were peeled off and the nakedness of his hands were revealed beneath. And then later, as they neared London Bridge, the man's movements were reversed. Charlie stared as smooth skin was covered, adorned, and anonymised by soft and supple leather. As he slid the gloves on, the man's face wore an expression of unhurried concentration. His eyes, cast down to his lap, looked almost sultry under the overhead lights.

And so Charlie had new details to add to the pictures developing in his mind. Almost by themselves, they had expanded into a dirty movie where the man who sat not-quite-opposite stroked himself with the same unhurried concentration—all while Charlie both watched and pretended not to watch.

Charlie shifted in his seat. Concealed by the hum of his laptop, his dick was aching, treacherously hard. At that moment, the man caught his eye. Charlie, unprepared, reacted clumsily. Rather than glancing away, he froze in place with his mouth hanging open.

He must have looked breathless; he felt breathless. The man with the briefcase did not look away, either. Instead, he held Charlie's gaze for a few moments and a knowing smile flickered across his face. While Charlie watched, he inched a gloved palm down his thigh. But when the glove reached his knee, the man reached down for his briefcase and stood abruptly to leave. The train pulled away from London Bridge with

Charlie still blushing, still struggling to understand what he'd just witnessed.

He struggled with it all weekend. Had he imagined it, that smile, that moment of understanding? During the day, while out with friends (drinks, tapas, cinema, then drinks again) he managed to put it out of his head. But at night, when it was dark and there was no one to stop him, he drove himself crazy imagining a gloved hand around a thick, hard cock. The anonymous man, self-possessed, quiet, as serious in his pleasure as he appeared in everyday life—did he know, did he want Charlie to watch? Shined shoes, dark suit, black gloves; the only flesh on show an obscenity. Charlie conceded the fight and came twice that night, and then twice again the next. He touched himself with care, calling to mind an attitude of unhurried concentration, a rippling smile on a familiar mouth. He eyed up a pair of leather gloves online but didn't buy them. The ones he wanted cost hundreds; he thought of them sullied with come and shot his own halfway up his chest.

On Monday morning they missed each other, and on Monday evening, too. Tuesday arrived bright but cool and Charlie met its chill with nervous anticipation. This time, the man met his eyes as soon as he took his seat. Charlie thrilled, shivered, and felt a little sick. The man removed his gloves and turned calmly to his paper. Charlie chewed on his lip all the way through to Green Park. There the man caught his eye again as he replaced his gloves and prepared to leave. Heat rose in Charlie's face—it was deliberate, it had to be. Wasn't it? The man left the train; Charlie stared after him. He did not look back, though Charlie couldn't think why he should.

The day dragged on, sluggish and unbearable. He told himself he was being ridiculous and that nothing was going to happen.

In the evening, he waited for the tube with a thundering pulse, knowing his hopes were pointless. They might not even be on the same train. And even if they were, what then? Charlie boarded and found his usual seat. When the train shuddered into Green Park, his dick was throbbing dully beneath his laptop.

Charlie rubbed the back of his neck and glanced over to the open doors. No one appeared. Or rather, a great number of passengers got on, but nobody that Charlie wanted to see. A man with a turban took the seat not-quite-opposite—he had a briefcase too but his was battered and shabby.

The disappointment cooled Charlie a little. He let out a breath and squared himself to his laptop screen, consoling himself with thoughts of an evening alone. A takeaway, maybe, and a good long shower with his imaginary movie for company.

The train slowed again and halted. There was movement next to Charlie: the elderly man at his side levered himself up to standing and shuffled off the train. Someone else replaced him; the pressure against Charlie's arm changed as they settled into their seat.

Charlie paid no notice. But then he glimpsed something and stilled. Was that a flash of black leather? He flicked his eyes to the right and saw an arm close to his, clad in beautiful dark felted wool. The arm moved, and the edge of a leather finger grazed Charlie's wrist.

All at once he was rock hard again; hot and sweating. He dared to turn his head and found next to him a well-cut profile, belonging to a familiar figure in a dark overcoat and gloves. A pair of frank grey eyes were directed towards him; above them, an eyebrow quirked upwards. Charlie swallowed, unsure what to do next.

The man gave him a smile, the kind which might pass between strangers who shared the same secret. Then, knowing he had Charlie's full attention, he went through his fastidious ritual. Each finger was loosened in turn as he teased the leather free; gradually, he drew the gloves down his wrists and off. It was as slow as a striptease and it made Charlie's mouth dry. He had no idea why it affected him so, but it did and he supposed there was nothing he could do except go along with it.

Neither of them spoke. The man went to lay the gloves in his lap and, by a careful rearrangement of his overcoat, displayed to Charlie the hard line of his cock beneath his trousers.

Charlie didn't know what to do. London Bridge was the next stop and the man would soon get off the train. A window of opportunity had opened, but no action he could think of seemed right.

Beside him, the man continued to read his newspaper in apparent peace. Charlie sweated under his jumper, unable to decide on *anything* and cursing himself for it. The train was slowing; London Bridge was approaching—but, miraculously, the man didn't ready himself to leave. The gloves stayed nestled in his lap, thrillingly close to the hardness beneath.

They travelled further east and the carriage started to empty. Still neither of them moved. North Greenwich arrived, Charlie's own stop, but he stayed put, fixed to his seat by something strange and unfathomable. More and more people got off. The train became quieter and quieter until they were alone in their section of the carriage.

It was then that the man made a movement, one sudden but smooth. He began to slide the gloves on again, as teasingly as he'd removed them. Charlie almost moaned out loud—at some point his own hands had become fists—but he was afraid, too. Was this it, was the man leaving? Had his inability to act pushed him away?

But even this thought couldn't break the spell he was under. It seemed it wasn't his choice to act. He was on a journey and being taken somewhere new—all he could do was wait for its end.

Without speaking, and without turning in his seat, the man offered his newspaper to Charlie. His eyes flashed with an unspoken question. Charlie took a breath, knowing he only had one chance to read the moment right. He slipped his laptop back into its case and set it on the empty seat beside him. Then he took the paper and opened it, creating a shield between himself and the rest of the carriage.

Calmly, as easily as anything, the man slipped his hand into Charlie's lap. It moved with slow surety, straight for its goal. Charlie tensed with anticipation and felt a soft pressure stroking the length of his dick. The glove caressed and squeezed, mapping out its shape through the warm denim of his jeans. Thick leather fingers slipped down between his thighs, prising them open and groping what they found there. There was no other word for it; Charlie bit off a gasp and spread his legs as much as he could. A leather palm lay heavy upon him. Charlie squirmed; his hips gave a little jerk and rustled the pages of the newspaper.

The train stopped. More people got off, a couple got on. Charlie watched them choose a seat at the other end of the carriage with a fast-beating heart. One chance, he thought. That's all. He dropped the paper across his lap and underneath its cover opened his jeans. He freed himself and then picked up the paper again. His dick was thrust up through the teeth of his open fly, eager for a gloved hand upon it. There was a small pause; the man next to him made a soft, considering, pleased sort of sound. Then, finally, the glove resumed its gentle, fondling attentions.

Charlie had to fight back a sigh of relief. The leather was cool against his heated skin; smooth-textured but at the same time rough, blunt-edged, and crude. The silent man at Charlie's side kept his touches light. He massaged rather than stroked and set his thumb to the plush head to rub soft circles against its wetness. Charlie had to glance down to watch and found, to his dismay, that the sight was too much. The leather made his nakedness that much more shocking; it looked debauched, clinical, and yet too intimate to bear. His cock jerked; its first eruption spurted messily across the gloved hand. Charlie had to let go of the newspaper on one side so he could bite down onto the heel of his palm.

His orgasm convulsed through him. Both he and the man watched his dick shudder and spit. Soon it was over, but the glove continued to work him, coaxing, knowing, slippery with his fluids. Charlie chewed on his lip as he struggled to regain control of his breathing. His come had pooled, dripping, onto the black leather and he desperately wanted to know what it would taste like from such a vessel.

And there were other things he wanted, too. Would the man let him watch as he stroked himself with his beautiful gloves? Would Charlie enjoy getting on his knees to suck him? He thought so—he particularly wanted to know how the leather would feel against his cheek...

But the doors were beeping open—the train had arrived at the end of the line. Before he knew what was happening, the man had upped and left, sweeping out with his briefcase and taking Charlie's dreams with him. The newspaper, concealing the mess he'd made of his jeans, was the only thing left behind.

Charlie blinked, bewildered. A desperate urge to rush off the train after him to follow overtook his senses. He wanted to find out who the man was and when they could do it again—but he was interrupted by a fresh horde of people boarding. Their noise and busyness forced him to confront his appearance. His face was red, he was still short of breath. He sat up, squaring his shoulders, and tried his best not to look like he'd just had the orgasm of his life.

Disappointment crested within him—but it soon subsided once his fevered mind began to cool and reset. He'd known that he'd only had one chance with the man on the train and he'd taken it. It was over and done with, something never to be repeated. He'd reached the end of the line.

But when he went to surreptitiously refasten his jeans, he made a discovery. The newspaper was not the only thing that the man had left for him. In his lap, slightly sticky and very used, was a gift—the pair of leather gloves.

Once Charlie got home, he cleaned them as best he could and then left them to dry. For a few days, he avoided them completely, aware of their presence but unsure of their power. He never again saw the man on the train and, after a week of looking out for him, Charlie accepted his fate without too much regret.

Because the gloves had been a gift—of that he was certain. The first night he used them on himself, he thought of him and wondered if he had pleasured himself like that, too.

Surely, thought Charlie, he must have done. He'd seemed fully aware of their attractions and he must have left them so I could enjoy them as well. Maybe he pictured that sometimes, even now, when *he* was alone.

The thought sustained Charlie through several entertaining evenings of self-discovery. And, over time, the man in his dreams changed shape. He was controlled, he was precise, he was patient—but he could've been anyone. Charlie started to search the faces of the men he passed in the street. Would any of them enjoy the gloves as much as he did? Was there anyone else out there in need of a man on the train?

One day, on a whim, he wore them on his way to work. They'd looked wrong with his usual jumper and hoodie, so he'd found an old bomber jacket to go with them instead. His reflection followed him across still-darkened shop windows and it pleased him. He looked like himself, but different. More self-assured, perhaps older. Perhaps not.

On the train, he noticed someone, a man of about his own age. He was reading something on his phone; there were earbuds in his ears. His gaze caught Charlie's gloves and lingered.

Charlie flexed his fingers and smiled. Was today the day? Would he reach the end of a different line?

If not, he knew it would happen soon. Chances were everywhere, on every train and in every station. It was a matter of knowing where to look—and what to do when you found it.

Now, Charlie knew.

2

Satori

The wind was getting up. Despite his tired legs, Aidan picked up the pace. Behind him, Dimitris's crunching bootsteps speeded up too.

The burn flowing along the centre of the glen was widening, an encouraging reminder that their gradual descent towards civilisation and safe shelter had begun. But the huge rounded mountains, ancient and worn, still surrounded them, and it felt to Aidan that there was a long way to go before they would reach it.

"Wait!" Dimitris grabbed Aidan's wrist, almost causing him to stumble. "That rock! There!"

He flung an arm out; Aidan twisted around to see what he was pointing at. The sun was lowering and the ridgeline above them undulated darkly against the sky. Below it, on the mountain, huddled the object Dimitris had seen. An irregular shape, well-camouflaged, but somehow out of place.

"Could that be it?" Dimitris said, half to himself. Without waiting for an answer, he charged off up the slope to investigate.

Aidan hurried after him, trying to shake off the stiffness

which had settled in his legs. Fourteen gruelling miles over difficult terrain had taken its toll, and the pause to argue about continuing their search had only worsened his aches. In the end, Dimitris's concerns had won—and rightly so, Aidan knew. It was less than two hours until nightfall and the mountain bothy they'd counted on as a back-up shelter was a good four miles from their current position. Visibility was already dimming so it was unlikely they would reach it by dark. With thick clouds rolling in, threatening snow and fog, it wasn't a smart move to risk getting caught out by the weather. Dimitris was right—they had to change their plans. Back to the village it was.

All throughout their discussion, Aidan had known that, yet he still hadn't been able to let go of his quest. Failing felt like just another thing for him to be disappointed about—something that Dimitris was aware of, too. He'd listened to Aidan's arguments with an astonishing amount of patience. Aidan had wanted desperately to find the cabin ever since he'd first read about it. Hidden in the bare hills of the Cairngorms, disguised as a boulder, an eccentric landowner has planted it there. Like a mountain bothy, it was open to all. Unlike a bothy, however, it was tiny—inside, barely a shepherd's hut—and unmapped. Anyone could spend a night there for free, but only if they were capable of finding it. That was the bargain—the rare kind that Aidan had been confident about keeping.

As it had turned out, his confidence had been misplaced. The late hour, the change in weather, and Dimitris's sensible nature had forced him to admit defeat. They had turned around and changed course for the village. But then, not long after, Dimitris had taken a single glance up and there it had been.

"You've fucking found it!" Aidan cried as he caught up with

Dimitris at the top of the steep, scree-filled slope. Nestled under a crag, a hundred metres above their heads, was a boulder that wasn't a boulder at all. Now he was closer, its oddness stood out. It was too rounded, too smooth. And its surface was too pale, lacking the weathered look of the old, old rocks nearby.

Dimitris let out a whoop as Aidan seized hold of his shoulders and pulled him in for a bear hug. Heavy rucksacks and the instability of the pebbles beneath their feet kept their celebrations muted. And once the cheering and the clanking of walking poles finally stopped, the silence was great. All Aidan could hear was their own breath, the wind, and the great unmovable stillness of the hills around them.

It felt like a secret door had opened. The thought crept through the hairs on the back of his neck, tightening his throat. They were going to spend a night on the mountain, somewhere hidden, somewhere few had been. It promised him a kind of magic: the isolation, the wildness, the blissful suspension of normal life. He could leave everything behind, here. Even if it was only for a night.

Almost reverently, they pushed on up the slope, picking their way across and up the edge of the mountain. Sometimes they walked upright, sometimes they were forced to scramble. They paused often to check their route. The going was hard, especially after their long trek, but after some minutes a faint path appeared. It was nothing more than a string of bare rocky patches linked by wiry, thinning grass, but they followed it with increasing confidence.

A few flakes of snow were falling when they arrived. The path petered out at a largish niche carved into the side of the mountain. One side was sheltered by a vertical rock face, while the other was open to the view and the valley below. The floor was level and carpeted with small stray rocks, heather, and some bedraggled grasses. The boulder-cabin was nestled perfectly in the middle, looking faintly uncanny, with sculpted concrete skin and an incongruous dark doorway cut into its side.

Dimitris strode straight over to the cabin, but Aidan hung back. Tension, relief, and joy were at war inside his heart. It was beating fast, and he wanted to savour this, their initial moment of discovery.

"There's a window here," Dimitris called. He was on the side of the cabin which overlooked the valley. Aidan watched him cup his hands around his face as he peered inside. "Can't see anything, though—there's something blocking the view."

They shared a quick glance; Aidan went over and saw that he was right. The window was a square patch of darkness, as blank as a sheet of black card.

Aidan sucked in a breath. "Better try the door, then, hadn't we?"

Tension was now winning his internal battle—what if, after everything they'd been through, the cabin was locked, or out of use? Or already occupied? Then they would have to turn back to the village after all.

Together, they moved back around to the entrance. A dark oblong hewn into the concrete made a porch about a foot deep; inside was a very ordinary-looking door and door handle.

Aidan put his gloved hand on it and took in a deep breath. "It's going to be bloody awkward if there's someone already in there," he said, trying to make light of his fears. "There's not enough room for the two of us as it is."

But it wasn't locked. The door swung easily open to display

a very empty cabin panelled in pale golden wood. A small skylight in the pitched roof, hidden from the outside, let in a little light. It was just enough to reveal a few dusty bootprints proving that others had recently visited. But, other than that, it was dry, clean, and bare.

Aidan let out a sigh of relief.

"Brilliant," breathed Dimitris, leaning over Aidan's shoulder to look inside. He gave him a small shove forward. "Come on, aren't we going in? I'm getting cold standing around."

Aidan unclipped his rucksack and slipped it to the floor. The sudden loss of its weight, and the unreality of finding a tiny house inside a boulder, left him feeling off-balance.

Dimitris followed him inside, his boots thumping on the wooden floor. While he looked around, Aidan kneeled by his bag and began unpacking his food and firelighting things. There wasn't enough space for them both to explore—the cabin was only just long enough for a tall man to lie down in. Even Dimitris had to stoop if he stood too close to the sloping walls.

There was a slim fuel-burning stove set close by the door. Dimitris bent down and examined it before moving on to a series of panels in the walls. They were fixed into place by metal catches. He undid some and let down a sleeping platform, which hung suspended on a couple of strong chains. Another made a table and revealed the blocked-up window. A square of fading sunlight was thrown from it across Aidan's lap.

"Wow, this place is cool," Dimitris said. "Look at this view."

Aidan crowded in behind him. In keeping with the cabin's proportions, the actual pane of glass was only a hand's breadth wide. From it, the entire glen—and at least half of their wandering, searching journey from earlier that day—was spread out before them.

Dimitris glanced back at him. "You're very quiet," he said. "You okay? Happy now that we're here?"

"Yeah." Aidan nodded, smiling. He felt giddy but peaceful. "A little stunned, I think. And thanks—for keeping us safe by making me face up to reality. And then for finding this place anyway."

"It was just luck," Dimitris said. "I looked up at the right moment, when the light was right or something. It's really well-camouflaged. But you knew it was here, somewhere in this valley."

"Yeah, but still," Aidan said. "I don't think I would've found it on my own." He turned away, back to the door which had swung closed behind them. "I'm going to let some fresh air in before you get that stove going. It's a bit stale in here."

Dimitris had dropped to his knees and was setting out kindling and coal for the fire. He gave Aidan a nod and carried on without looking up.

The darkness outside came as a surprise, as was the flurry of wispy snow which hit Aidan's face when he went out. Gone were the greens and browns of the hills. Almost all of the colour had leached from the landscape, leaving everything blue, black, white, or grey. Aidan stood breathing in the cold damp air. He used his body to keep the snow from blowing into the cabin, watching the paler shades of the land and sky dim. The clouds seemed to hang heavy, swirling low and thick over the mountain above. He waited until he heard the crackle of fire behind him and then firmly shut the door against the night.

Inside, it was now dark enough that torches and lamps were necessary. While the cabin warmed up, they dug out some extra-warm fleeces to wear and then hung up their outer layers to dry. Half an hour later, they had water hot enough for tea and Aidan brought out a handful of chocolate raisins for them to share. After that, they had enough energy to set up their quarters for the night.

They were used to roughing it in cramped tents, so sharing a tiny cabin was not something that they'd expected to present a challenge. But they soon realised that fitting both of them into it for sleep was not going to be easy. With the sleeping platform down, there was not quite enough room for the other to lie on the floor. But the platform itself was obviously designed only for one.

Dimitris eyed it at length. "I mean, it's not ideal," he said. "But I think we can both fit. I'm shorter than you, I can wedge myself into that recess in the wall."

Behind where the platform folded down was a small ledge a few inches deep. It seemed intended for torches and other useful nighttime items—not for fully grown men.

Aidan scratched his head. "Unless one of us could sleep underneath?" he said. "Like bunk beds."

Both of them squatted down to look. The clearance between the floor and the platform above was enough to fit a prone human body—but only just.

Aidan grimaced. It would be like sleeping in a particularly shallow coffin.

Dimitris looked similarly unimpressed. He straightened up again. "Look, I'm happy to try sharing if you are," he said. "It'll be warmer, too. But if it gets too uncomfortable, one of us can try the floor. We'll just have to sit up a bit to avoid burning ourselves on the stove."

"Fine," Aidan said. "But if you push me out I'm going to punch you in the balls. Because that floor is not going to give me a soft landing."

Dimitris laughed. "Bet we're so knackered neither of us moves all night, anyway."

Before going to bed, they ate a meal of instant noodles and rehydrated pork and beans. As the candles and fire both dimmed, they grew more and more tired. Eventually, their conversation dried up and came to a complete stop. Hungry as Aidan was, his sleeping bag called so loudly that it was a struggle to keep his eyes open and finish his food. Yawning, they shuffled into their sleeping bags, fully dressed.

Finding a position they were both happy with was tricky, but once they'd settled it wasn't too bad. Dimitris, as far as Aidan could tell, went straight to sleep. But Aidan found himself lying awake in the dark, hyper-aware of the hidden nature of the cabin and the wider wildness of the mountain outside. It was as quiet as anywhere he'd ever been. He closed his eyes and listened, wondering if he was only imagining the hiss of falling snow as it covered them with its soft blanket.

Now that he was there, inside the cabin, he couldn't take it in. Also, he was too warm. Dimitris was pressed hard against his side, with his knee in Aidan's ribs. Aidan undid his sleeping bag a little and rearranged himself, laying his arms on top to feel the cool air. His head ached with tiredness, but his mind was crowded and wouldn't let him rest.

The coal in the stove still had a faint glow, its light only bright enough to highlight the darkness. It gave a small pop and then, with a quiet rustle, subsided.

That morning they had started at dawn, striding through the eerily grey landscape with a cold northerly wind in their faces. A train had brought them up the night before to stay at a walkers' hostel close to the start of their route. Aidan had plotted it meticulously—it had taken months for him to piece it together. He'd studied maps as diligently as any cartographer, had pored over the clues and photos left by others online. Planning the search for the cabin had taken up much of his spare time. What was he going to do now it was over? Just go back to his depressing, everyday life?

In the hostel bar, they'd toasted themselves with whisky and had shared easy jokes with the other guests. From the outside, they seemed to be heading out for nothing more than a bit of a lark. No one watching would have guessed they had deeper reasons to venture out into the mountains.

Though they'd never discussed it, Aidan knew that walking provided them both with a comforting fiction; a feeling that, as long as they could carry what they needed on their backs, they could just keep on going. Every step they took seemed to lead them further away from their day-to-day lives.

Sometimes Aidan liked to pretend that he didn't have to return at all—maybe Dimitris did the same, he didn't know. He had more reason than Aidan to play those kinds of games. He'd recently lost his brother, whereas Aidan was just lost. Nothing he did seemed to work out; all his early promise had been spent. Work was both menial and meaningless, he'd failed in love, he was a disappointment to everyone except Dimitris. He was even a disappointment to himself. When he'd witnessed the worst of Dimitris's grief, Aidan had wondered if he was grieving for something too. If so, he had no idea what it was.

Every day he felt a little more useless, surplus to requirements. Sometimes, he knew, his mind was not a good place to inhabit alone. So he liked to explore other places instead. That was why he enjoyed being out in the hills and mountains; why he enjoyed the challenges and rewards of bagging peaks and camping out in the rough. It was also why he'd spent all those long evenings scrolling through forums looking for clues to the cabin's whereabouts. And why he hadn't been able to give up on finding it, even when he'd known it was the right thing to do.

Whenever he got drunk enough, Dimitris would say that that was what he admired about him: that Aidan didn't give up. He kept going. No matter what.

They knew each other so well, now, better than either of them would likely admit to. They'd seen the best and worst of each other: Aidan the dreamer and Dimitris the realist. What a pair.

Aidan blinked into the darkness, sensing rather than seeing the wooden walls of the cabin protecting them from the elements. Dimitris's body heat was leaking through his sleeping bag, but this time he was glad of it.

It was funny how things turned out, he thought. All of that planning but, in the end, it had been Dimitris who'd found the cabin. Without him, Aidan never would have made it. And without him, it wouldn't have been so much fun.

* * *

Aidan woke from a sleep so deep it felt enchanted. Dimitris was watching him, propped up against the wall by Aidan's feet, with his sleeping bag wrapped snugly around his chest.

Dimitris grinned. "Think we're in for a cold one today."

Aidan rubbed his eyes and sat up. Everything hurt, particularly the bony parts which had been squashed against a wooden board all night. And the rib which had become so well acquainted with Dimitris's knee. But the light soon distracted him—muffled and diffuse—and he remembered the snow of the night before. He looked up at the skylight to find it was white over, so thick and soft that the sun appeared to glow through it.

The fire had long gone out so their first task was to relight it. Then they gazed out of the square little window. The glen below was carpeted in deep snow and the mountain opposite reflected the brilliance of the sun's rays. It was beautiful, magical. But reality hit Aidan and he remembered that they had to get back off the mountain to the village and its hostel.

"Do you think we'll get down okay?" he asked.

Dimitris shrugged. "We've got all day to try," he said. "I'll make a sledge out of my rucksack if I have to." His face showed no concern—in fact, he looked almost energised by the prospect.

Aidan laughed at him. Now he'd moved farther from the depths of his dreams, he saw that Dimitris was right. Going down would be much less work than coming up. And once they'd made it down to the glen, they could use the burn to navigate out of the hills and back to civilisation. From there, it was only three miles to the road and a warm hearth.

"God, I love snow," Dimitris said, still gazing out of the window. "Don't you?"

Instant porridge and tea soon warmed them, helping to prepare them for the day ahead. Aidan stretched his feet out towards the crackling fire while he sorted out his feelings. Their imminent departure was conflicting him. On the one hand, it would be nice to eat a proper meal and sleep in a proper bed. On the other, it seemed like they'd only just arrived and he wasn't sure if he was ready to leave the cabin yet.

Dimitris turned to Aidan with a mischievous look in his eye. "Hey, you know what we could do?"

"No," Aidan said warily. "What?"

Dimitris didn't answer straight away. Instead, he went over to the door and peered out. When he closed it again, he was grinning to himself.

"We could snow bathe," he said.

Aidan blinked. What was Dimitris talking about?

"There's no one around—and we could both do with a bath." Dimitris paused for a moment, then started to undress with abrupt, decisive movements. "Did we really come up here just to leave again?" he said. "I don't think so—we came here to do something we wouldn't normally do, be people we don't normally get to be. So I'm going, even if you aren't."

Aidan watched as he shed first his fleece and then a long-sleeved wool base layer. "You're actually going out there, naked?"

"No, I'll have boots on," Dimitris said. "And underwear. Don't think my junk will like the snow as much as I will."

Aidan snorted in disbelief. "But it's freezing—"

"Look, they do it in places like Norway, don't they?"

"Yes, but after a sauna," Aidan countered. "And they go back in it, afterwards."

Dimitris finished hopping out of his thermals and cast a glance around the cabin. "Well, with that fire going like it is and a hot drink waiting for us, I reckon we'll be okay."

"'Us'?" Aidan said. "So now I'm coming, too?"

"Come on," Dimitris said. His mischievous look was back again, accessorised this time with a smile. "You know you want to. We found the cabin, didn't we? And now we've got to do something daft to remember it by."

"Fuck's sake," Aidan complained. But he stood up and began tugging off his top. "Fine. Five minutes. Then you're giving me one of your packet soups. And some chocolate. *And* you're making me a cup of tea."

Dimitris pulled on his boots and opened the door. He was a ridiculous sight: naked but for his briefs and heavy walking boots; chalk-white and goose-pimpled with cold.

But the scene behind him was wonderful—a white world sharply edged in black. Everything was utterly still, perfect and untainted, like an illustration in a book of fairy tales. Aidan forgot the cold, forgot everything else. He came to the door, mouth held open, breath suspended. He could've been a child again, someone young and innocent of life's disappointments.

"Yeah, you're right," he said. "We'll never get to do this again, will we? Not in a place like this."

Dimitris opened the door wider. "Well, here goes."

They were hesitant at first, and silent—but then something overtook them and they were running out like school kids to dive into the snow. The shock of cold was overwhelming; Aidan resurfaced with a painful gasp, his lungs bursting fit to drown him. But as he struggled free, pure euphoria swept him up in its embrace. Dimitris barrelled over and with a roar took him down again. Aidan grabbed fistfuls of snow and rubbed them into his hair.

They tussled fruitlessly for a while, laughing, then broke apart to repeat the cycle. Aidan had no idea how long their snow-fight went on for. Fevered and joyful, they knocked each other down and got back up again, until their skin was a brilliant, painful crimson. Then, once the cold had penetrated deeper, they rushed in unison, giggling and shivering, back into the cabin.

The warmth of its interior, combined with the warmth of their exertion, flushed them with an immediate surge of heat.

Every muscle in Aidan's body seemed to lighten. He swivelled where he stood, gently took hold of Dimitris's shoulder, and pressed his lips to his cold and smiling mouth.

Dimitris did not freeze—and, belatedly, Aidan realised that he'd expected him to. Instead he gasped, very quietly; an inhale of breath that Aidan felt against his lips.

And then he kissed Aidan back.

From Aidan came a sound, low in his throat. When he'd reached for Dimitris, there hadn't been a thought in his head beyond demonstrating a wordless sort of appreciation. He opened his eyes, which had instinctively fallen shut. Dimitris was pulling away but he was watching Aidan intently, waiting for something. His face was serious, still close to Aidan's own.

What was he waiting for? thought Aidan. And then he realised and smiled; and suddenly he was pushing Dimitris back towards the sleeping bags which lay still rumpled on their makeshift bed.

Dimitris sat down heavily on them and kissed him again, no longer hesitant. It was easy, so easy. His tongue slid alongside Aidan's own and he pulled Aidan down astride his lap—Aidan had to clutch at him for balance.

He felt Dimitris's hands stroking his sides, warm and gentle and tender. Something rose in him, something unfamiliar and powerful—was he going to cry? It was blissful, naive, ragged at the edges. He gasped and found it was natural to thrust his hips forward and down; to meet Dimitris's on the way up; to drive their mutual arousal on towards its end.

Once it was over, there came a strange but comfortable silence. Aidan unhooked his legs from Dimitris's hips and shuffled clear so that he could sit up. But Dimitris didn't move. He lay where he was, sprawled out on the sleeping bag, unselfconscious of both his nakedness and the come staining his underwear.

Something was ringing in Aidan's ear, an emotion or an inkling of an emotion, something he couldn't yet identify. Whatever it was, it was loud and truthful, but it didn't frighten him.

"What was that about?" he asked, as much of himself as of Dimitris.

"Dunno," Dimitris said. He was looking at the ceiling, his face thoughtful but free of alarm. "I did say we should do something daft."

Then he turned his gaze back to Aidan, suddenly sincere. "I don't think I need to know what it was. Not yet, anyway. But it was good and I don't regret it."

Aidan considered that and the adventure he'd had that weekend. Finding the cabin after almost not finding it; the snow and the snow-fight. Dimitris arguing with him and then kissing him. Gasping into his mouth as he came.

Nothing had changed and everything had. It felt like life. Like a real life, one lived fully. Like the clouds had parted and given him a brief glimpse of enlightenment.

Maybe he wasn't wasting his life, after all?

After they'd packed up and roughly swept out the cabin, they left it behind with little ceremony. It wasn't necessary, Aidan realised, as he headed with Dimitris back down the slope. The cabin had done what he'd needed it to do. It had freed him of something; he was unchained.

Maybe he'd found something, too.

By his side, Dimitris smiled. Aidan smiled back, ready for the new adventures that awaited them at the bottom of the mountain.

It was funny how things turned out, he thought. All of that planning but in the end, it had just been Dimitris. Without him, Aidan never would have made it. And without him, it wouldn't have been so much fun.

3

Of Camaraderie and Corruption

The tranquillity of the Earl's rooms was shattered irrevocably the moment its occupant returned from his walk. Spencer, instructed by his lord to remain behind, had kept himself only lightly occupied and had spent a blissful hour availing himself of the books which lined the Earl's apartments. But then a great noise had burst in upon his peace—the door had slammed and the shout came for wine—and so Spencer leaped up and went with haste towards his master's voice.

The scene he discovered in the bedchamber was an assault to the senses: brilliant candlelight, dutifully tended to by Spencer, illuminated the silks, satins, and gilt which adorned both the furnishings of the room and the three men within it. Present were Lord Godolphin and Viscount Marlborough, two recent arrivals at court and current favourites of the Earl. Amongst the servants, Spencer had heard much uneasy whispering about their dress: the heels of their shoes were too high, their wigs excessively elaborate, the buckles and buttons of their clothing gaudy and glittering. But it was hard to say exactly what about their *manner* so disturbed. For they were bold and daring and witty, and had just as many admirers as detractors—and yet their presence in Lord Harley's bedchamber brought Spencer a great unease. Though created of such flimsies as scent, powder, and liberally-applied rouge, their essence dominated so that, in comparison, the very candlelight itself seemed dim and the space around them appeared plunged into shadow.

His lord, the Earl of Harley, was by no means unfashionable—indeed, no calf was more well-turned and no profile more admired—but the companionship of Godolphin and Marlborough had wrought a change upon him. The difference was not so much one of dress—French fashion he continued to take in moderation—but one of mood. He seemed more volatile and his passions more quickly inflamed. Though he had never been chaste, propriety had always had its place in his character. But now, even as Spencer approached with the claret, his lord had thrown all that asunder and was busy indulging the scandalous attentions of Lord Godolphin.

Spencer set the tray down close by the fire and concentrated upon safely unburdening its contents. On the rear wall, a shadow flickered, one of his master and Godolphin which loomed high and grotesque. The Viscount appeared at Spencer's side and helped himself to some wine to sip, idly watching that which Spencer strove to ignore. Spencer turned to depart, quickly, but found that it was beyond his powers to avoid glimpsing at least a part of his lord's activities. He had leaned in, his attitude commanding, to assert his claim over Godolphin's painted, preening mouth. Spencer averted his eyes and hurried away.

He was almost at the door when something behind him clattered to the floor.

"Spencer," called his lord, breaking briefly from his occupation. "Get that, will you."

Spencer did as he was bid. Godolphin had seated himself in Lord Harley's lap, and in the process had abandoned his cane. Spencer returned swiftly and, stooping to collect it, tried to put from his mind the unnatural glisten of Godolphin's mouth. It was brash, berry-bright, and being enjoyed far too lewdly by his master. He laid the cane on a low table and once more prepared to leave the room.

But his blushes were not to be spared. Indeed, it appeared that Lord Harley was in a confrontational mood and wished to provoke them.

"No, bring it here," he demanded abruptly. His thighs were spread to take the weight in his lap; Godolphin's buttocks, clothed in tight satin, nestled cosily across them. "It has a very interesting feature which I wish to make use of."

Both of them had turned towards him; Marlborough's snigger could be heard from across the room. Spencer, as composed as he could be, stepped towards Lord Harley and laid the cane into his waiting palm.

"Here," Lord Harley said, "I will show you."

The handle was bulbous and silver but free of the embellishment which Godolphin was famous for. Lord Harley twisted the handle and it came loose; a few more turns unscrewed it clean of the cane. He held it up to Spencer's gaze. The rounded silver knob which formed the cane's handle was revealed to be the tip of something greater. The whole object was a solid four inches of undulating silver, which up until then had lain hidden inside the stick.

Lord Harley brought it to his mouth and kissed it in triumph; laughter filled the room from all sides. Spencer remained silent.

"I had it made especially for me," Godolphin said. Supported by Lord Harley, he leaned closer to Spencer, his voice soft and purring. "What do you imagine it is for?"

Spencer knew his lord's proclivities well and felt he could imagine its use accurately enough without explanations. "It is very ingenious, my lord," he said, addressing his bow towards Godolphin. "And most amusing as well. I congratulate you on your whimsy."

"Whimsy is one way of putting it," observed Marlborough drily. Having refilled his wine glass, he had circled closer and now plucked the item from Lord Harley's hand. "Though I wouldn't describe it thus."

Lord Harley's lips were twisted in amusement. "Nor would Godolphin. He takes his pleasure more seriously than that."

All three were caught up in their fun; Spencer, temporarily forgotten, prepared once again to withdraw. His lord's attentions had been drawn back to Godolphin: he had a greedy hand spread across the front of his breeches and seemed ready to take ownership of what lay beneath. Marlborough had settled into a nearby chair as if waiting to enjoy a particularly ribald play. No one paid him any notice.

But then Godolphin shrugged off his coat and set to work loosening his neckcloth. Rather than wait for his lord's instructions, Spencer darted forwards and picked up the discarded garment. The coat was a sugared-almond shade of lavender, exquisitely fine and of the best silk. Spencer shook it free of creases and then, almost automatically, took from his lord's hand the long expanse of lace that had made up Godolphin's neckcloth.

"I hear your lord's reputation is under constant discussion at court," Godolphin said to Spencer. He tilted back his head, exposing his throat to Lord Harley's mouth. His tone was conversational but his gaze carried a challenge. "Apparently the company he keeps is, at times, a little suspect. What say you of that?"

"I say nothing at all, my lord," Spencer assured him. "On the few occasions I've observed my lord in company, I have seen nothing to trouble me. He has seemed quite content and that is all I am to worry about."

Lord Harley lifted his mouth from Godolphin's neck and said, to no one and everyone, "Spencer knows me truly. He knows I would not forget his loyalty should it ever come into question." His hand, now plunged deep inside Godolphin's breeches, began a course of vigorous explorations.

Godolphin gasped; his hips bucked. Spencer carefully averted his eyes from the fluid, rippling sheen of his breeches. Though ivory-coloured, their appearance was not in the least innocent.

"You may leave us, Spencer," Lord Harley said. "But don't stay away long—we will soon want refreshment."

Spencer gave a nod of gratitude and turned away. He left Godolphin's clothing, still warm, on a nearby ottoman and fled back to his book.

Twenty minutes later, he creaked open the door. The scene beyond had altered. Godolphin was now the one lounging on the sofa, having helped himself to claret, and it was Marlborough who occupied his master's lap—thankfully, still clad in his breeches. Lord Harley's face was hidden from view. He had reclined backwards onto the bed and seemed to be entirely unaware of Spencer's presence. Spencer judged that the refreshments would keep a little while longer and silently moved to withdraw.

Godolphin, however, prevented him. Spotting Spencer, he called out, "Here! You! We need more wine! And some food, too!" He sat up and thrust aloft the hand holding his empty glass—his shirt, half undone, slipped down over his shoulder.

Spencer bowed and went to obey. When he re-entered with a laden tray, the figures on the bed took no notice of him and he endeavoured to do the same for them. But Godolphin leaped up and refilled his glass, near snatching it from Spencer's hand as soon as he set the bottle down.

"I saw you spying at the door," Godolphin said, close to his ear.

Spencer stared at him in shock. Godolphin was grinning, his wine-stained lips pulled back over his teeth. The rouge which had covered them was smeared; with his darkened brows and pale powdered face, he looked quite savage.

He took hold of Spencer's shoulders and twisted him around to face the bed. "What do you think of your lord, hmm?" he asked. "Is he not everything which is desirable?"

Forced to look, Spencer saw much which he had previously tried not to see. The scene had progressed since his last visit. His master's coat was gone and his waistcoat hung open. His shirt was gathered up by his neck, bunched tightly in Marlborough's fist, and his stomach was bared to Marlborough's depravities. Except for a tightly-laced corset, Marlborough's torso was quite naked. Below it, his cock stood out stiff and proud, and his eager movements thrust it repeatedly against his lord's skin.

Spencer couldn't speak. Godolphin, enjoying himself, continued with his questioning.

"Is he not a fine figure of a man? You must know *that*—I expect you see more of him than even Marlborough and I."

Godolphin pushed him closer. Their presence surely could not escape Marlborough, but he was too intent on his pleasure and did not turn. The shaft of his cock slipped gleamingly over his lord's stomach; pale satin clung stubbornly to the globe of his behind as it rocked into Lord Harley's still-covered lap. All was pink and creamy gold in the candlelight.

"You are very quiet for a peeping Tom," Godolphin accused. "Are you perhaps overcome?"

He followed up his query with a crude and sudden grab for the contents of Spencer's own breeches. Spencer froze utterly, so appalled that he could not find the words to protest. And, worse even than Godolphin's groping fingers, was the knowledge that he would find there at least some evidence to support his argument.

"Quite a sizeable mouthful," Godolphin said appraisingly. "No wonder he keeps you around."

Spencer made no response—the corrupt vision before him was too distracting to bear. Details assailed him: his lord's hair coming loose from its ribbon, his mouth blurred with Godolphin's paint. Bite marks on his chest, just beneath Marlborough's fists. And Marlborough, strenuous in his riding, with his back arched and his head tipped back. His swollen flesh rubbed insistently over Lord Harley's firm and glistening stomach. A sudden realisation presented itself to Spencer—that Marlborough, following closely in Godolphin's path, was soon to empty himself over his lord. And that his lord was going to enjoy it.

"If you must keep him standing there, Godolphin, at least let him be useful." Lord Harley rolled his head to one side; his eyes were fever-bright but showed signs of annoyance. "Spencer, take down my breeches."

Godolphin chuckled lightly and whispered to Spencer. "Now you'll get what you want—and a very intimate view, at that."

Spencer did his best to ignore both him and the nature of the task he'd been given. Really, it was no different, he attempted to tell himself, from the usual nightly assistance he provided to his master.

As he approached, Marlborough stopped and rose to a kneel. He gave no other sign that he knew Spencer was there, and Spencer set quietly about dealing with his lord's breeches. The folds at the front were distended by his arousal, but unbuttoning the waistband and then peeling them down was no more trouble than when Lord Harley had imbibed too much wine. His lord's cock, thick with lust, was freed; Spencer had only a momentary impression of its musky heat before his duty was done.

But then he paused, remembering that no servant's work was ever truly complete. "My lord," he asked, "shall I unbuckle the knees also?"

Lord Harley's impatient huff could be heard before he spoke. "Yes, of course," he said, leaning around Marlborough to rebuke Spencer. "I won't serve these gentlemen well with my legs tied together, will I?"

In response, Spencer flushed. But he applied himself doggedly to the task, finding that the buckles were not so simple to undo now that Marlborough had resumed his activities. Above him, the length of Lord Harley's member slid easily along the crease of Marlborough's satin-strained buttocks. Spencer, slipping the last buckle free, frowned to himself—he could easily see what his lord intended and yet Marlborough had not moved to undress. He hoped he was not expected to do *that* as well.

Godolphin had positioned himself on the bed by Lord Harley's head and was watching with interest. He, too, had divested himself of his breeches and bent to whisper something into his lord's ear. Lord Harley gave a bark of laughter and struck Marlborough hard on the flank.

Marlborough dismounted. His chest was aglow with his exertions, an appearance markedly at odds with his unnaturally white face. Beneath the corset, his cock still rudely stood; a small wet stain had been impressed upon its satin.

All three of them looked over at Spencer, who, having finished removing his lord's shoes and breeches, had been nervously waiting to be dismissed.

Lord Harley arranged himself into an attitude of patience, with his hands pillowed behind his head and his legs crossed at the ankles. He still wore most of his shirt and waistcoat, and his white silk stockings still clothed his legs. His cock remained hard and obviously wanting—a clear bead of fluid sparkled diamond-like at its tip. All of this was novel to Spencer, yet it was his patience that surprised him the most. He was not accustomed to it and had expected his lord to treat his companions in the demanding manner he knew well. Lord Harley was waiting, supine, obviously requiring their attentions—and yet they were both leaving his side and coming toward *Spencer*, while his lord looked tolerantly on.

Each took one of Spencer's arms; he was pulled up to stand at the foot of the bed. They pulled at his hair and clothing while Lord Harley fell into deliberation.

"I don't know," Lord Harley said doubtfully. "I'm not sure he's enough to tempt *anyone's* fancy, is he?" He gave a great sigh. "But maybe you're right, maybe the two of you can make something of him."

"Harley, how *wicked* of you," Marlborough said, drawling out his false concern with glee. "And with the poor thing standing right here, listening to every cruel word."

Godolphin sniggered and joined eagerly in. Together they burst into a chorus of chastisement which had Lord Harley as its target. First, they petted Spencer and made a show of providing comfort for an insult he hadn't felt. Then the undressing began, accompanied by covetous fondling and teasing pinches. His coat was removed, and his waistcoat and shirt. Spencer, shivering in his breeches, limply let them. He wasn't sure what else to do. His lord was watching, his cock still at a fine stand, and whatever this was it was obviously his wish. Marlborough was busy powdering his dark hair white; Godolphin had engaged upon blackening his lashes and rouging his cheeks. One of them went to his lord's wardrobe and procured a fine cut-away coat, which they proceeded to dress him in.

"*Don't* listen to him," Marlborough was saying. "Don't pay him any attention. He wouldn't know a pretty young man if one sat on his cock."

"He's just jealous that you've got such a lovely big prick," agreed Godolphin. "*Much* bigger than his, and I'll bet it lasts longer too."

Lord Harley laughed; Spencer stared at the floor. The coat was a delicate pastel blue, one of his lord's finest, embellished with silver thread and tiny glittering gems. His own plain neckcloth was removed and a gauzy lace one was tied around his throat.

"Now," Godolphin was saying, "here is an opportunity to show him how wrong he is."

"Yes," agreed Marlborough. "A very great chance."

Spencer, bewildered into submission, said, "But how? What am I supposed to do?"

"Why, finish undressing him, of course," Godolphin said. "Look, I'll help."

Lord Harley had risen to his elbows. Godolphin kneeled on the bed beside him and pulled his waistcoat back over his shoulders so Lord Harley could slip it free. "Now you take care of his neckcloth."

Spencer's heart was in his mouth as he faced his master. Until then, it had been his own humiliation which had occupied him but, so near to Lord Harley, the very real danger of his situation gripped him. There was no telling what his lord was thinking or what he might do next. Spencer avoided his eyes as he sought the ends of his neckcloth, as prepared to be mauled as someone forced to pet a tiger. But nothing happened. Lord Harley simply tipped back his head to allow Spencer to wind the cloth free, leaving Spencer no choice but to continue with the charade he'd been helplessly dragged into.

He undid the remaining buttons on his master's shirt and removed it. Next, he slipped to one knee, and Lord Harley, now sitting regally at the end of the bed, allowed him to untie his garters and slide off each of his stockings.

Movement flickered above him. Spencer looked up to find Marlborough and Godolphin leaning eagerly around his master. Lord Harley raised a leisurely hand and settled it onto the back of Spencer's head. Its warm pressure was steady—quite gentle, in fact—but Spencer bucked in surprise, skittish as an unbroken pony. A heavy silence fell, one which seemed to span an unbearably long moment, but which in reality lasted barely a tick of the clock on the mantelpiece. The expectant faces of Marlborough and Godolphin loomed closer.

Spencer dropped his gaze to his master's cock, which strained towards him as hard and as commanding as the man himself. When he took it in his mouth his only feeling was one of shame that he had not held out longer before reducing himself to such an act.

Lord Harley gave a long, low sigh; he spread his legs a little further apart and held Spencer down on him longer than was comfortable. Once released, Spencer coughed the breath back into his body but then plunged on with his task. He told himself his aim was to get it over with—for once his lord found completion, surely he would be done with him? But he found his tempo slowing almost against his will. For it seemed that he liked it: the smooth round head pushing past his lips, slippery with his lord's burgeoning pleasure, and the intrusion filling out his cheeks. Shame-filled, resentful, and yet aroused, Spencer performed for his lord, with his lips and chin wet with spit and his own cock growing to fullness.

Soon, Lord Harley stopped guiding him, and Spencer was left to do whatever he wanted. With eyes tightly closed he sucked, choked, and swallowed; his eyes watered; static buzzed over the blood pounding in his ears. Lord Harley groaned unguardedly and Spencer grasped himself through his breeches, knowing that even that little might cause him to spend.

The shocking knowledge he had to confront was that mortification was making his pleasure greater. His world had shrunk to the use that his mouth had been put to, a use he'd submitted to and was glutting himself upon. His breathing was laboured to the point of claustrophobia; so hard had he pushed to swallow his master's length, he'd almost reached the limits of his lungs. The straining in his breeches did not cease; a slick bitterness had coated his throat and he knew what would soon follow. A sick desire for this, and for an increase to his shame, caused him to finally open his eyes. He expected to see his master looking down at him, triumphant, perhaps gloating at the downfall of his loyal servant and ready to paint his signature across his tongue.

But that was not what Spencer saw. Instead of revelling in domination and tyranny, Lord Harley was engaged in much the same activity as Spencer himself was, and just as eagerly. Marlborough and Godolphin had each presented him with their hard, curving lengths and he was pleasuring whichever of them he could reach. Often, that meant both at once—it appeared to be a competition between them to see who could occupy the most of his mouth. Lord Harley certainly offered no preferences—he remained dumb throughout, greedily lavishing attention on whatever was offered to him.

Spencer wiped his chin and noticed with affront that his lord did not seem to mind the loss of his mouth. He reacted not at all, even though he had been about to find his release in it only moments ago.

"Poor, dear Spencer," Marlborough said. "*We* noticed your efforts and very admirable they seemed. To be frank, I did not think you had such skill at your command."

Spencer frowned at him. Some of the fog brought on by his terrible lust had cleared and now his chief emotion was one of irritation.

"I quite agree," Godolphin said. "You can put that mouth into my service any time you like. But what you must understand is this: no matter how skilled your silky throat, the Earl here is quite lost to anything once he undertakes the same task." He gave a little thrust of his hips and, as if to illustrate the point, Lord Harley impaled himself deeper upon Godolphin's endowments with a sharp whine. "Not so frightening like this, is he? Give him a good hard prick or two and he's ever so eager to please."

Spencer wanted to deny that his lord had caused him any fright, but there seemed to be no point. He had no pride left to defend. He watched Lord Harley caress the plush tip of Godolphin's cock with his flickering tongue. Spencer's aching had not lessened and the sight, though angering him obscurely, did nothing to temper it.

"But don't lose heart," he heard Marlborough say, "for he is not done with you yet."

Something was rolled across the bedspread towards him—the bulbous silver tip of Godolphin's cane.

"Your lord's satisfaction would not be complete without exhausting every avenue," Godolphin said. "And I do mean *every* avenue. Look in the pocket of that fine coat of yours."

Spencer's fingers closed around a small sharp-cornered object. He brought it out and saw it was a jewelled snuff box which he had never before seen—presumably either Godolphin or Marlborough had secreted it there while dressing him. He opened it and inside found, rather than snuff, a kind of ointment.

"I never go anywhere without my own special preparation," Marlborough declared. "I'd be lost without it—you'd be surprised how it comes in, even when strolling quite innocently around the gardens of uninteresting English nobles. One isn't safe anywhere, any more—it's exceedingly shocking."

Spencer wasn't listening. He looked first at the items in his hands, and then at the newly prone form of the Earl. His legs were spread asunder and his chest was heaving. His cock lolled heavily against his stomach, wet still from Spencer's mouth.

"You know what to do, don't you, Spencer?" Godolphin coaxed. "Consider it a reward for your tireless and devoted service, this evening and every other."

Spencer thought back over his day, and over the hours and days before that. The Earl, though not the worst master he knew of, had not treated him as a true gentleman should. He had endured numerous condescensions, had been put through many difficult moments, and had been made to suffer endless put-downs and humiliations. The current hour, he saw, was the climax of a pattern that had begun long ago.

Reward? he wondered. Or a still greater punishment? He could not tell but was sure he was damned either way.

He rose up from his knees and, taking hold of his lord's legs, roughly pushed them further apart. Quickly, he smeared the silver object with Marlborough's preparation and pressed the tapered end to the entrance of Lord Harley's passage. His lord gasped thickly around Marlborough's cock; Spencer watched his body tense and recoil, vindictively hoping that he found it too cold for such an intimate area. But the metal warmed rapidly and soon his lord adopted a more welcoming posture. With a minimal amount of teasing and twisting, Spencer was able to slide it fully inside him.

Lord Harley sighed and shivered—but the rest of his reaction was lost to Spencer for Marlborough withdrew from his lord's mouth and, with a long low cry, brought himself off over his face. Lord Harley moaned a little at the sensation, blinked, and then calmly reached for Godolphin. Spencer watched wordlessly. He seemed to have become quite numbed to the sights before him.

Marlborough sat back on his heels while he caught his breath. Then he turned to address Spencer. "What do you think of your lord now?" he asked with a grin. "Suits his new face paint, doesn't he?"

Spencer did not answer. Arguably, he was now a member of their strange little grouping and as such could do or say as he wanted, but he still did not feel able to respond. Besides, the preparation Marlborough had given him had somehow got all over the part of the object which was not buried inside Lord Harley and he needed to concentrate. His lord was writhing back against Spencer's hand and he did not wish to lose his grip.

Marlborough leaned close, his expression critical and assessing. "Be careful not to deny yourself," he warned. "Don't wait too long or that which should be yours will be spent without you."

He twisted suddenly over to one side, his hands busy with something on his person which Spencer could not see. But soon he re-emerged, holding a strip of pale blue satin frilled with lace. Spencer realised he'd removed one of the garters holding up his stockings. Marlborough looped it around the base of Lord Harley's cock and tied it gently with a bow.

"What a pretty little harlot," Marlborough said, considering this absurd picture. He flicked his eyes up to Spencer's and held them. "You *do* know what harlots are good for, don't you, Spencer?"

Spencer started, struck less by Marlborough's words than by the certainty that he was going to follow through on them. Everything else that evening had happened as if in a dream he had no control over. So if there was any reward to be found, he would take it while he still had the chance.

He flew to a stand, fumbling with his breeches. Lord Harley was sprawled below him in an attitude of wantonness; silver winked between his thighs. Spencer drew it out of him, none too gently, and thrust himself into its place.

Lord Harley gasped in shock. He abandoned his pleasuring of Godolphin and scrabbled out with his hands, twisting them into the sheets. Spencer leaned his weight into him and felt his length glide deeper. A glance downwards brought his heart into his mouth—he watched as his lord's body received him until he was enveloped entirely.

The Earl groaned; his head rolled back upon his neck—but then he bucked and made as if to grab hold of Spencer. Godolphin and Marlborough each took an arm and pinned him against the bed. Spencer remained where he was, sheathed but frozen. The whites of Lord Harley's eyes stood out and his nostrils flared. It was a moment again fraught with danger—but it passed. Lord Harley, relenting, lay back and offered up his body; and Spencer, emboldened, set about taking his dues.

The act came to him more naturally than he'd expected. Lord Harley's body was pure heat; for Spencer, all was sensation and his pleasure so undiluted that it hovered close to pain. The experiences of his evening consumed him—inside he was burning, fuelled by all he'd been put through. Belatedly, he realised Godolphin and Marlborough were watching intently, observing in silence the results of their ploys and cajolements, their mouths and eyes heavy with lust. Spencer cared not. He put a knee up on the bed, hooked his lord's leg around his waist, and fucked his openness without further consideration.

The punishing rhythm soon pushed Lord Harley too far—his lace-adorned cock jerked as it showered his chest with release. But Spencer kept going. He felt as if he could keep going forever. His senses, his passions, were so heightened that he seemed above every other concern.

Not so Lord Harley—though the band of lace and satin kept him at a stand, the effect was obviously artificial and he wilted, even if his cock couldn't. Weakness overtook him; his arms and legs sagged and his flanks shook from their sustained efforts. Even his arms, long freed from his friends' grip, quivered with fatigue.

Godolphin sighed and petted Lord Harley's disarranged hair. "Such a brave, beautiful harlot."

Spencer's rhythm did not falter; Lord Harley squirmed feebly as another pulse of spend left him. Marlborough leaned over to scrutinise his torment.

"Think he's got one more in him?" he asked Godolphin.

"I put my trust in Spencer," Godolphin said. "I'd wager no more than thirty to one against."

Spencer found their chatter easy to ignore. Lord Harley's teeth were gritted—the weakness had left him and he was all tension once again. His hands had clawed their way to Spencer's shoulders and his fingers clung on painfully. His thighs were taut, gripping Spencer's hips like a vice. And his gaze, directed up at Spencer, communicated a clear command: don't stop.

With every thrust of Spencer's, he flinched and floundered; his groans and shouts grew louder. Sluggish bursts of pearlescent liquid pulsed from him, and each brought him closer to his goal. Smiling, Spencer swiped a finger through the mess and fed it to him. Lord Harley sucked obediently, moaning at his own taste. His prick, artificially swollen, shiny with spend, slapped hopelessly against Spencer's stomach. Spencer ignored it in favour of pinching his nipples hard. It brought about a cry which was closer to a sob and coaxed from him another trickle of viscous fluid.

He knew their climax was nearing. His own was tied inextricably with that of his lord, and it was clear that his lord could not stand much more. Heat seared between them—all was slick sweat and desperation. Harley's face was wrought with exquisite agony, his mouth pulled open and his expression reaching, ascending. Spend still streaked his cheeks. *He is beautiful,* thought Spencer—his lord, how he worshipped him.

Harley's hands were grasping, pulling at his arm; Spencer sprang forward to capture his mouth, his kiss vicious and plundering. Teeth caught on his lip, a tongue filled his mouth. Harley groaned, a sound quite different to the breathy accompaniments of his travails—it was sudden, sharp, and final. He shuddered in Spencer's arms; a final perfunctory release flowed from his cock, thick and white. With a growl, Spencer pressed him flat to the mattress and spent noisily inside him.

His rest was not long—Harley's chest was heaving beneath him, hot and sticky and uncomfortable against his own. Spencer raised his head to take in the sight of him. He was naked as a babe, wet with sweat, and striped with the spend of three different men. His dark hair was patchy with powder, his face defiled. Rouge was blotched across his mouth and remnants of Marlborough's release still clung to his skin. He did not speak; his blue eyes were wide and searching as he gently unfastened the cloth around Spencer's neck.

Spencer followed the actions of his hands with his own. Harley's fine, strong fingers knew their task well and it always pleased him to be at their mercy. When it was done, Spencer pressed a gentle kiss to his lips and, taking possession of the cloth, began to wipe down Harley's face.

A noise beside them drew their attention. Marlborough's lust had been reignited and Godolphin was bent over for him.

They watched idly before Spencer shed his coat and Harley freed himself of his intimate, but deceptively useful, decoration of satin and lace.

Then Spencer lay with him, making himself a cover for his body. "My dear Harley," he said, and kissed him deeply. "You were magnificent. Quite horrible. I hope you didn't find any inspiration in me?"

Harley smiled sleepily. "You said you wanted me to be horrible, so I was. It's as simple as that."

"And you were rewarded quite satisfactorily?"

"If you'd rewarded me for any longer, I might now be dead," Harley replied. "Finished by my lord's passions. Is that not a fitting ending for so devoted a servant as I? Maybe you'd like to try it next time—I'm sure I could continue to be horrible to you if you wished it." He spoke with the bright sparkle of amusement that Spencer loved. There was no better companion for him than Sir Harley, lifelong friend and most trusted advisor to Lord Spencer, Earl of Tonbridge.

Spencer laughed, kissing Harley once again. "Were you seen in the gardens? Did anyone guess you were not me?"

"We managed to keep at a distance from the others who were out walking," Harley said. "I do not think we were spotted."

More sounds interrupted them—Godolphin had just reached his completion and Marlborough soon followed. They collapsed in a heap, laughing and panting, each preening ridiculously for the benefit of the other. Spencer, observing them with fondness, called out to them.

"What is this scene of dreadful corruption before me?" he said. "What a pair of harlots! I do believe the Earl is to blame—apparently, the company he keeps is, at times, a little suspect. What say you of that?"

Marlborough roared. Godolphin sat up, straightened his wig, and said haughtily, "I already miss the lowly Spencer—he is so much more obliging. And whatever he thinks, he doesn't dare say."

"But as an Earl he has his charms," Marlborough said. "You can't pretend you don't find them considerable. After all, we've all seen the evidence with our very own eyes."

Godolphin dropped his manner and laughed. "Nor can I pretend to mind being called a harlot," he said. "I think it suits me abominably well."

"I think none of us can refuse the label," Harley said, blinking up at the ceiling. "Our camaraderie is very distinct in its nature."

Marlborough smiled knowingly. "And even more distinct between the Earl and yourself."

Harley blushed, quite prettily. Spencer enfolded him more securely in his embrace and said, "And speaking of scenes, I thought our little play very successful—perhaps there is scope to arrange another act?"

"There you are, Godolphin," Marlborough said. "The servant Spencer shall ride again—and maybe you shall get to make use of him next time."

Spencer laughed. "Perhaps," he said. "It is not written yet, after all."

4

Inside Looking Out

Today I had sex for the first time in *months.* I almost thought I'd forgotten how. There were two windows and several metres of cool night air between me and the couple living opposite, but we managed it.

Though last year—when things were normal, when going outside wasn't a big deal and when I could fuck anyone any time I wanted—would it really have counted as sex? Would it have felt so good? I don't know. But it was like they were here with me—I could almost feel the blond one's mouth on me. And one day soon, when lockdown's finally over, I know I will for real.

I hadn't noticed my neighbours until recently. The first time happened by chance; I glanced over at their window and caught them unawares. Even then I didn't immediately know what I was seeing. Or where it was going to lead me.

Our flats are in identical blocks. They line up perfectly, so that when I stand at a window it's as if there's a mirror between our buildings. The sun was particularly strong on the afternoon I saw them. It was high in the sky and their window was filmed with dust and reflected shards of light. In it, I could see the blue of the sky, and plumes of white cloud, and an indistinct form which I soon recognised to be that of a man.

He was half in shadow, half brightly lit; shirtless and turned away from me, so that all I could see was his back. His jeans—or trousers, or whatever they were—had been pulled down enough to hug his thighs. Above them, his bare arse curved firm and full.

It would have been his movements that caught my attention, I think, for it was obvious that he was not alone. Someone else was kneeling in front of him, with his dick deep in their throat—or so I imagined, as I couldn't actually see them. But the smooth, rolling motion of the standing guy's hips was enough for me to make an educated guess. I might've glimpsed a bowed head down there or the tensed length of a pale throat. Or I might not've.

At the time, I assumed they were unaware that they could be seen—though now I know they were not that innocent. I watched until the man moved suddenly; his arm jerked up to clutch an unseen head and he threw back his own. The muscles of his back tautened; his arm flexed as he held someone in his grip. I hadn't meant to watch, but it was already too late to do anything about it. And I was familiar with those small actions of dominance—the fist in the hair, the unleashing of an unannounced orgasm. In my own experience, those who liked to be on the receiving end were to be admired. I wondered who it was and what they were to him. I pictured another man, but that was just my own selfish preference. Either way, I'd enjoyed the show.

Then a hand stretched upwards, curling loose and languid around the other's hip. The man standing bent down a little, to speak or react to the person on the floor, and a brief moment passed between the two of them which I couldn't see. When the one on the floor stood and finally revealed himself, I caught a glimpse of honey-tinted hair and a satisfied, playful expression. That was all: he took his lover's hand and pulled him deep into the flat, out of my sight.

I didn't get off on it, not that time. Sadly, I was out of the habit—sex on my own had become dull and I was tired of it. Like a lot of people who'd ended up in lockdown alone, I'd spent a lot of time online, but virtual sex had soon lost its shine. If you ask me, it's a lot of work without much payback. Porn is easier—low effort, always there when you need it—but that's also part of the trouble. No spontaneity, no to-and-fro. Always chasing echoes of what you could once have had in person. It couldn't replace what I was missing, what I really wanted.

Take my neighbours, for example. Everything about them had seemed fresh and urgent. The images they'd left me with were as vivid as a centrefold spread, even though they'd shown me half as much. I remember wondering if they'd just met, that maybe I'd just witnessed an illicit, newly-illegal hook-up. But then I remembered the familiarity of that hand pulling the other into the flat. Into, I presumed, the bedroom that they both must share.

Before, I hadn't been particularly conscious that anybody lived opposite. These buildings are so anonymous. Until I'd seen them through that window, the block of flats next to mine was just a big, blank building—theoretically inhabited, but no more real to me than that. Having moved into my flat just in the nick of time—about a fortnight before the shit hit the fan, in fact—I hadn't been there long and my attention, like everyone else's, had been distracted. I'd been inside, if you see what I mean, but I hadn't been looking out. And neither had I realised that others might be able to look in at me.

But, after that first glimpse, I started to get regular sightings of them. Much clearer ones, too. I saw them cooking in the kitchen, eating together, watching TV in the evenings. In my defence, there was—and still is—nothing else to look at. The view from my flat is pretty much entirely of theirs—and they have made themselves very noticeable. Others have blinds or curtains, but my neighbours rarely decide to shut the outside world out. It became difficult not to notice that, when I made tea in the mornings, they were perched elbow-to-elbow at their kitchen table. Or that when I had taken myself into the spare room to lift a few weights, they were working at separate desks just opposite. Sometimes, they'd stop what they were doing to turn around and talk, and I would stop, too, and watch them. Though their expressions were dulled by the distance between us, body language is easy to read and I could see how much they enjoyed each other's company.

I liked getting to know them, to be honest. It was something new to interest me, like a TV show which had been left on in the background. Every so often, I'd raise my head and be briefly caught up in their story. I started to understand the routine of their lives, and to wonder more deeply about their characters and personalities.

When I went out on the balcony to smoke—an old habit I seem to have picked up again—I'd quietly study what I could see of their flat. It's identical to mine, set at the top corner of a long edifice of fake bricks. Our buildings have rows of huge windows and each flat has a tiny, precarious-looking glass balcony stuck onto it. Their bedroom, I guess, is like mine and faces out towards the railway tracks, but I have a decent view of the rest of their flat. They have a lot of plants, which seem to need frequent watering, and piles and piles of books. Their balcony is laid out carefully with colourful pots and a single chair, but it doesn't get much use. Too windy, I would say, and definitely too small to be comfortable—I've only used mine for smoking.

I've got to know them as individuals, as well. The one who'd stood at the window is fairly tall, mid-thirties—I think—and dark-haired with straight black brows. That's about all I can see of his face but the rest of him looks pretty good. He carries a touch of bulk in all the right places. Framed by light and shadow in the window, he'd been like one of those luscious statues that the ancient Greeks were so fond of—the way his plump, round ass had glowed in the buttery afternoon light could've moved anyone to poetry. He's often restless, I believe. Like me, I think he feels hemmed in. When taking a call, he paces up and down. And while he waits for the kettle or the coffee maker, he opens and closes drawers for no reason and drums on his thigh with a teaspoon.

The other is far more serene, and, from what I can tell, likely to be considered beautiful. He might be younger, too. He's smaller and slighter, with golden, or maybe sandy hair, which he's allowed to grow long. I would say that he's not my usual type, but the way he moves is really something. You can tell he's a great fuck just from watching him cross a room. He seems conscious of every single one of his body parts. Now, so am I.

As I went about my long, empty days, I thought about them often. My work was on hold but I was still getting paid. I had nothing to do. I tried to tell myself not to worry, but I still felt it gnawing at me. I work at a gym and I'm usually busy, active, surrounded by people. My life seemed not-quite-real. I had to mark time like a prisoner, with regular smoke breaks, an hour of exercise, maybe a spot of morning sunbathing by the window when the weather allowed. I went for runs and at home I got stuck into my weights. That was it. My body felt efficient and strong, but machine-like. On pause. Until they gave me something else to think about.

I had to wait a couple of weeks to see them fuck again. Back then I still thought that the first time had been an accident, so one night at dusk, when they drew their living room curtains, it didn't occur to me to wonder what they might be getting up to behind them. It was hot that day and, in an attempt to catch what little breeze there was, all my windows were wide open. I lay limply, flopped across my sofa in front of the TV, but it soon held less interest for me than what was going on outside.

Behind the curtains, a bright light was switched on. Then they appeared: two shadows projected across their screen of white curtain. There was no warm-up act, they just got straight into it—and that was what jolted me out of my lethargy. One was bent over a piece of furniture, the other lined up behind him. Though technically they were hidden from me, I could pinpoint the exact moment of penetration. I felt it almost like I was there with them—the momentary hitch, the gasp, the shuddering intensity of sensation. And then the straining apart of legs—hamstrings drawing tight, inner thighs stretched—and the impact, the heat, the slapping rhythm of two bodies moving together.

Their window was open so I listened hard in case any sounds reached me, but none did, even when they both came. I heard them in my mind, though, and before I could question the morality of it I'd watched the whole thing with a hand shoved down my pants. But when I considered it again, it occurred to me how staged the whole thing was—like theatre, a live show just for me.

I thought, though, that they probably didn't know *I* was watching. I thought that they just liked the possibility of being seen—by *anyone*. But it was still a lovely idea. I kicked my jeans off, tipped my head back, and came all over my stomach. I was loud, too, as a sort of thank you to them—the first proper orgasm I'd had in weeks. Good, deep, and cleansing, it was. And I had a strange feeling that they wouldn't mind if they overheard.

Not too long after that, we started to interact in a neighbourly kind of way. Our balconies were too far apart for conversation, but the dark-haired one caught my eye while he was outside watering the plants. It was my regular morning smoke break and I gave him the automatic, stoic sort of nod that politely acknowledges another person's existence.

He nodded back.

And then, because we had acknowledged each other once, we had to do it again. And again. Until somehow, about a week later, when he decided to clean the windows in the smallest, tightest pair of speedos I have ever seen, it seemed more natural to me to go outside for a smoke, than to stay in and watch from my kitchen while pretending I wasn't.

On the way out, I stripped my t-shirt off. The sun was full on me and I supposed that it was only fair that he had something good to look at as well. I angled myself away from him and lit my first cigarette as he stretched and reached and bent. Every so often I threw nonchalant glances in his direction; the muscles of his arms were nicely defined, though they were no match for mine. Once or twice I caught him looking, which was gratifying, and I decided it was okay to settle my gaze on his dick for a few seconds. It was very nicely packaged, full and round and perky, encased in smooth deep-blue fabric. He had a nice mouth, too, I thought as I lit a second cigarette. I could imagine it around me, wet and shining. And the way he'd tilt his face up to swallow me down with diligence—all part of a pretence that he was doing me a great, great favour. I've had a few guys like that and it was always fun when they dropped their defences and really let themselves go.

I was deep in my imaginings when the other slipped up beside him. He slung an arm around the dark-haired one's waist and kissed him sweetly on the cheek. He, I decided, would alternate between skilled and deliberately sloppy, and he'd feel entitled to every inch I had to give—and then some. I'm certain he has plenty of choice of which cocks to suck, though, so I can't say I blame him. I rather like that, anyway. Enthusiasm and a bit of attitude always go down well with me.

My neighbour abandoned his efforts at polishing the window and instead manhandled his boyfriend into an extremely possessive embrace. The blond one was also wearing very little, just a pair of shorts and a mesh vest of the type usually seen in gay clubs. I watched them kiss, all open-mouths and promises. They shared a few words; the blond one smirked prettily. His boyfriend grinned back, and then raised his head to smile at me, too. His hand lay on the blond one's arse. He squeezed it gently, as if assessing its ripeness, and the look he gave me invited me to assess it with him.

Well. What was I supposed to do? I turned so that I faced them, leaning on the glass balustrade and carrying on smoking as I waited to see what they would do next. The dark-haired one palmed the front of his speedos, fondling himself openly; keen to show me what he had tucked away in there. They had my interest: I threw my cigarette to the floor and ground it out. But the blond one whispered something in the other's ear and they went back inside—though not without a long glance over their shoulders at me.

It was still early and the sun was in the wrong place to let my gaze go with them into their flat. It was deep in shadow; I squinted hard but couldn't make out any movement within its depths. *My* flat, however, was lit up like a Christmas tree. I considered it over my shoulder; the end of the sofa closest to the window was bathed in light. It would be perfect for a little sunbathing.

So, in full view of anyone opposite who cared to watch, I lay down and jerked myself off. I knew they were there, somewhere, hidden in the darkness of their flat. I thought about them watching me while they touched each other, unseen, and I found the idea strangely moving. I hoped that the dark-haired one was fucking the other—it had definitely been implied that he would. And I'll bet it was glorious to watch.

Even though it was just me and my hand, I enjoyed it thoroughly. I had kicked off my sweatpants—I'd been working hard on my legs and it would've been a shame not to show them off—and, at first, I simply played with myself. I squeezed my dick softly, teasing myself unnecessarily and making it squirm in my hand. From my view, my dick looked good: long and thick and curved. I had the taste of smoke in my mouth, ashy and bitter, and the memory of the dark-haired one's staged possessiveness and pride.

When I came, I thought of them both in their flat, discussing me. I decided that they wanted me to fuck them both and what tipped me over was the idea of the blond one watching me make his boyfriend come. In my daydreams, he was overjoyed, and so turned on, lying just as I was, lazily stroking his cock while he waited for his turn.

Later that day, when they were back at their desks and I was once again wondering if I should try to pick up some private clients of my own, I remember thinking how glad I was that they had each other. They seemed to fit so nicely together. I would even have gone so far as to say that they were good for each other, though I'd never actually met them and was in no position to judge such a thing. But the observations I'd made seemed enough on their own. When they settled down in the evening to watch TV, I did the same, and it was almost like we were all in the same room together.

After that fun and eventful morning, they seemed to start actively looking out for me. Some of it was simple and friendly—a wave, a smile, a nod. Slowly, our lives started to converge. If I went out for a smoke, one of them would be taking a coffee break in the kitchen. Or I would come back sweaty from a run, just as the blond one rolled out a yoga mat. I would stand by the window to drink my protein shake. He knew I was there and he let me know it, giving me little smiles and glances and showing off his supple, pliant strength.

Once we caught each other in just the right mood. I applauded his efforts by rubbing the front of my running shorts. My cock was hard for him; he came over to the window and, leaning on the frame, gave me the most beautiful lingering look. Then, without breaking his gaze, he dipped his hand under the waistband of his leggings and tugged himself a few times. I think I actually moaned aloud—god, I wanted to fuck him so bad. He looked so tempting standing there, framed in the window with his hand working his cock—like something in a display case.

But he pulled his hand away and mouthed something at me through the window. I couldn't understand what he was saying at first, but eventually I got there: *"tonight".* He disappeared and came back with a pad of paper. I watched him write on it with big sweeps of his arm. He held it up, flat against the glass, and it said, *"10pm?".*

I agreed, though I wasn't entirely sure what was going to happen at ten or why we had to wait—both of us were already raring to go. His boyfriend was in the flat, I knew, and presumably could join us, or not, as he wished.

It was short-sighted of me, really, in retrospect. It all made a lot more sense once dusk fell and the lights started to go on.

I watched the little dabs of colour flick on all over town: a constellation of red dots wherever cranes towered, the blinking light on top of the Canary Wharf tower. I kept my own flat dark. I wanted to be sure that I could see whatever was going to happen opposite.

My neighbours had had an unremarkable evening. They'd followed their usual pattern of cooking, eating, and television. I tried not to keep looking at them, in case it seemed like I was hurrying them or something. So I answered a few emails I'd been avoiding and got to grips with my beleaguered finances. When ten neared and they got going, I was caught off guard.

First, their living room lit up, bright and stark as a football pitch. My blond friend came over to the window, shedding clothes as he went. He stood right up to the glass and peered out through his cupped hands, gazing into the depths of my flat.

Me, I realised belatedly. He was looking for *me*.

I ran over to the light switch and snapped it on. He stepped back and, smiling, slipped off his underwear. He was hard already; he slid his hand over his length a few times as he looked at me. His boyfriend appeared behind him and, kissing his neck, bent him forward so he was braced over a coffee table.

Both of them had their eyes fixed on me. My heart leaped into my throat—I hadn't expected such a sudden start to the evening and I felt unprepared. The dark-haired one was taking his clothes off, so I began undressing as well. But I wasn't quick enough—he was balls-deep in the blond one before I'd even started unbuckling my jeans. I watched their movements: slow, deep, undulations; the dark-haired one serious and steady; the blond one with his mouth gasping open and his face flushed. He kept rubbing his nipples, and when I took my cock out he moaned so very beautifully. It must have been loud, but I couldn't hear it. I could only see his face and his wanting.

I stroked myself for him, as close to the window as I could get; as near to him as I could get. His boyfriend gave me a smile—a quick, knowing smirk—and leaned forward to slip his fingers into his mouth.

I groaned and tightened my grip on myself. The blond one went deep on his boyfriend's fingers; he licked and sucked and moaned as though there was nothing he enjoyed better. He was working his boyfriend's dick, too—arching his back, grinding, making a show of how much he liked it. The dark-haired one smirked again and gave his arse a playful slap. He met my eyes as took charge of his hips, fucking him with vigour.

I'm not sure how long we spent there, all three of us moving as one. I kept time with them, stroking my cock in long, quick pulls, and they kept time with me. All the while, I thought about how useful that long blond hair would be for holding onto. I knew it would feel good wound around my fingers.

I came with my hand flat on the window, like I was reaching

out for them. I'm not sure what triggered it: the blond one reaching between his legs to touch himself or the dark-haired one groaning and grinding and staring at me like he wanted to swallow my dick whole.

It hit me hard; I had to lean on the glass, so my come ended up splashing across it. That happened by accident, rather than by design, but my new friends seemed very appreciative.

Soon we were all spent and sticky and panting. We said our goodbyes; the dark-haired one waved, the blond one blew me a smiling kiss. I felt peaceful for the first time in ages. Our lights were switched off and we went back to our own separate lives, only mine seemed less solitary than before. I went for a shower, and jerked off again, just because I could.

Some of their magic seemed to have rubbed off on me. I felt back to my old self, the one with a sex life to envy—exactly like theirs, even during a pandemic.

Little did I know the truth. Because I suppose I'd thought that they were like that all the time, whether I was there or not. I hadn't questioned the view I'd formed of them. Why would I have done, after all I'd seen?

And then this morning, I found a note in my letterbox downstairs. It was handwritten and it said:

Dear Hot Neighbour,

We just wanted to write and thank you for all the entertainment you've provided us with.

It's not been easy for us these past few months. My boyfriend has an autoimmune condition so we've been isolating since before lockdown began. I don't know when we'll be able to get back to normal—probably not even when restrictions start to end. Certainly not enough so that we can "enjoy" ourselves with others like we used to. It's been ages and we'd almost given up hope of feeling like our old selves again.

So when you moved in opposite, we really couldn't help but notice. Especially when you seemed to have a few very fun evenings at your laptop by the window... And we decided to repay you in kind :)

That's why I wanted to write and thank you for cheering us both up—we haven't "enjoyed" ourselves much recently and it's been just what we needed. Once all this is finally over, we'd love to invite you round.

And, in the meantime, we hope to see you again soon—usual place, usual time?

Your very horny neighbours,

Sam (and Emilio)

PS: Really hope we've got the right address! I've left you our flat number so you can let us know.

PPS: I'm the blond one :)

PPPS: Oh yeah, feel free to bring a friend to "meet" us when you feel safe having anyone over—we really love company :)

I've already responded, of course. I couldn't have that sweet blond bombshell—Sam—thinking he'd got the wrong flat.

And of course I couldn't pass up the opportunity of spending more time with them—in fact, I gave them my number. I suggested that we "enjoy" adding some acoustics next time we "met".

It's so nice to know I'm not the only one inside looking out.

5

The Price of Admission

The room was crowded with warm bodies and happy, preoccupied faces. At the bar people stood six-deep; a chain of hands ferried drinks through the crush to friends waiting at the back. Everyone was hoarse from shouting over the music. A large group seated near Ash erupted in roars of greeting as even more joined them.

Ash watched nervously from the sidelines, trying to look like he belonged. It wasn't easy being alone in such a place. He'd found a corner to wedge himself into, right at the end of the bar, where he hoped Omar would be able to find him. In the meantime, he'd been trying to catch somebody's eye. *Anybody's.* Just someone to have a friendly word with—a smile or a joke about how busy it was or how hot. But no one had paid him the slightest bit of attention. *Not one person.* Everyone seemed to be so caught up with their friends and their fun that he was completely invisible.

Once, a hot hand had gripped his waist, and a swathe of sweat-sticky skin had rubbed across his arm. Ash's senses had thrilled. Was someone interested, were they going to offer to buy him a drink or, better still, to show him around? But it had only been an accident. The man had pushed by on his way to the bar and Ash had been left staring after his leather-strapped back. He'd watched until it had been swallowed by the crowd.

Where was Omar? he wondered. For something to do, he took a swig of beer, though it was no longer cold and beginning to taste sour. He was thankful for it, anyway. To be alone and drink-less would have been much sadder than simply being alone.

"Another?" said a voice.

Ash looked up, startled. The voice had seemed curiously distinct among the clamour, but he saw it had only been the barman who'd served him earlier. He was waiting for Ash to respond, holding a chilled bottle of beer.

Ash sloshed the remains of his around in its bottle. "Thanks, but I've still got some left."

"First time here?" the barman asked. His face and his expression were loose and light, as if he'd recently breezed in from a day in the country. Instead, he'd been enduring a hot and noisy shift—Ash felt quite exhausted and he'd done nothing more taxing than prop up the bar for half an hour.

"Yeah," Ash said tightly. "It is." He was flushing, he realised with horror. Was it so obvious that he was new to this kind of thing?

"I thought I didn't recognise you," said the barman. "Look, this one's cold—I'll open it for you. Compliments of the house."

Before Ash could react the barman had reached out and handed it over. Ash took it automatically, his mind busy—*is he hitting on me or is he just being nice?* But by the time he'd caught up with his thoughts, the barman had gone.

"Thanks!" he called after him.

The barman was busy filling glasses at the other end of the bar and didn't seem to hear.

Ash took a sip. It was cold and very crisp and tasted better than his first bottle had—though he was so hot that anything would have been a relief. He drank some more and thought again of the barman. His eyes had been pale and very calm, like pools of still water. As he'd reached out with the beer, his long dark hair had spilled across his shoulder. He'd been smiling, too, with a sort of twist to his mouth—hadn't he? Ash blinked and tried to remember, but he couldn't think past those pale eyes shining oddly in the club's darkness. There was something about them that—

A sudden, sharp pain distracted him from his thoughts. Someone had stood on his foot: a woman, he discovered, with a heavy platform heel. Though he'd yelped and yanked his foot away, she hadn't bothered to turn around to apologise. She hadn't even seemed to notice. Sighing, he picked up his beer and limped away.

Pressing through the crowd, he made for the cavernous room at the back of the club. He'd caught a glimpse of it when he'd first walked in, packed with moving bodies lit by strobes of coloured light. The sheer number of people had made it seem impenetrable.

Now, observing the jostling mass of people, Ash regretted not making more definite plans with Omar. It had sounded so easy, so casual, so exactly the right thing to just agree when Omar had said, *"see you at Spank on Friday night?"* But Ash hadn't reckoned on one crucial fact, something he hadn't known when he was airily pretending he was familiar with fetish club etiquette—phones were not allowed. Not in the bar, not on the dance floor, and certainly not anywhere else.

Ash gazed into the crowd and reflected on his lot. With the luck he was having, if he tried to check his messages, he'd end up being kicked out. Should he go searching for Omar? Could he pluck up the courage to look in the dungeon downstairs? But he wasn't sure if that was an invitation-only kind of place. Ash imagined a long, snaking queue and a rubber-clad girl with a checklist guarding the door. Like in a nightmare-ish anxiety dream, he saw himself turned away, humiliated.

Better to start in this room, he decided. Now that he was closer, it looked a lot more like a normal nightclub, only with a very different dress code. Some people were dancing and the rest had settled in their own little groups. All were talking, posing, prowling.

Ash watched with rising frustration: everyone seemed to know each other. Omar was a regular—if he'd met up with him as they'd planned, he could've been in the middle of one of those groups, enjoying himself. Instead, he was standing awkwardly on the sidelines, obscure and uninteresting in his boring black jeans and vest.

Clutching his beer bottle, he edged around the room. The one advantage to being invisible to everyone there was that it should be easier to explore. Along the walls, he found nooks and crannies arranged with seating where a few public scenes were taking place. Small gatherings had formed to watch and Ash ended up on the periphery of one. A hooded man was chained up inside a cage and the woman to whom he presumably belonged was demonstrating something to her audience. It involved a rope and a specific sort of knot. Ash couldn't hear very well, but her friendliness gave him a lift of hope—and it crested even higher when a man on the other side of the crowd smiled and waved.

Ash started, but instinct checked him before he responded. A quick glance over his shoulder revealed what should have been immediately obvious: the man had been waving at someone behind him.

Without a clear idea of where he was going, Ash drifted away from the group and pushed deeper into the room. The emerald beacon of a fire exit sign glowed up ahead. When he reached the doors, he saw a dimly-lit stairwell behind them, and arrows pointing down towards the dungeons and to a smoking area somewhere outside. He went through; the stairwell was cool and the lighting soft. It was quiet, too. When the doors shut out the thumping music behind him, the relief was like a splash of water to the face.

He paused and took a few deep breaths. Away from the sensory assault of the dance floor, he could think clearly again. But noise and laughter soon returned to disturb him. The doors opened and a trio in squeaking rubber emerged, talking loudly in voices cracked from shouting. Ash watched them disappear in the direction of the smoking area. How pathetic he must seem, he thought. Hiding in an empty corridor, alone. It was hardly a night out to remember.

He drained the bottle of beer that the barman had given him and set it down at the edge of one of the stair treads. There was another sign above his head, one that he'd missed. It read *"Bathrooms"* and pointed upwards. For the lack of anything else to do, he followed it, and as he climbed he formed a plan of resolve. In the privacy of a bathroom, he realised, he would be able to check his phone. And then he might find a message from Omar, telling him where they could meet. It was silly of him not to have thought of it before.

And if there isn't a message, Ash thought, I'll just tell him I'm at the bar. I'll wait for one more beer, but if I don't find him by then I'll chuck the whole thing in and go home.

The stairs were irregular and winding so that, once at the top, Ash wasn't sure which direction he was facing in. To his left stretched a long, low, and rather dingy corridor. And the corridor to his right took a sharp turn, culminating in a pair of swing doors. There were no more signs directing him towards the bathrooms, or indeed to anywhere else.

He chose the long corridor and crept down it, unable to shake the idea that he was trespassing. The quiet was intense and the sound his feet made on the floor was far too loud. Its edges were thick with dust and the air had an unused smell. He came to another pair of doors and opened them cautiously, fearing that he was about to burst into a staff room. But on the other side there were only more stairs, leading up from below. A sign on the wall told him only that the bathrooms were back the way he'd just come.

He retraced his steps back to where he'd started and took the other corridor. Beyond its sharp turn and swing doors was yet another corridor, a shorter one, which smelled of damp plaster and had a high ceiling stained with water damage. There was also another sign, indicating that the bathrooms were up ahead. But underneath something else was written in faint letters: *"New Admissions"*.

Ash frowned, ready to ignore any distractions, however mysterious they might sound. Now that he had a plan, he wanted to follow it through. But halfway along the corridor was a door which was not quite shut and light of a strange quality was spilling from it onto the uncarpeted floor. The back of his neck prickled but he peeked inside. The eerie light was explained easily enough. The storeroom, for that was what it seemed to be, was full of old mirrors. They were hung or propped against every wall, reflecting the wan light of a single bare bulb dangling from the ceiling.

He stepped inside to look around but it seemed to be empty. Odd, but definitely empty. It was only when he turned to leave that he noticed some paper stuck to the back of the door with a scrap of yellowed tape. Something was written on it in ink.

"WELCOME," it said. "All new admissions are invited to use this space. One at a time only, please. Keep the door closed when the room is in use."

Ash blinked and re-read it, but it didn't make any more sense to him the second time. There was nothing in the room except mirrors. Some were framed, some were unframed. Many were so old that they were spotted or silvered, but all of them looked cheap and unloved. He walked round again, noting a rough circle of freestanding mirrors set out like sentinels in the middle of the room. Their placement was disconcerting; they seemed almost to be waiting for something. He eyed them nervously, but then told himself that the room was no longer in use. The carpet was threadbare and dirty and the sign on the door was almost illegible. No one had been in here for a long time and whatever the room had been, it was obviously that no longer.

He turned to leave and, out of the corner of his eye, caught a glimpse of movement. He whipped around, his heart pounding—and then realised with a laugh that it had only been his reflection passing from mirror to mirror. As if to prove to himself that he hadn't been spooked, he went over to the nearest one and inspected it. It was a normal, if slightly dusty, full-length mirror. He circled round them all, weaving a path in and out until he arrived back at the door. There he paused, with his eyes fixed on the empty space in the middle of the room.

Then, without knowing why, he shut the door with a firm click.

Nothing happened. Everything was still. If there was anyone at all in the same part of the building, they must either be dead or asleep. The corridor outside was complete in its silence.

Ash moved away from the door and into the space in the middle of the room. The view there was strange but not unexpected—something like an infinity mirror, only more jumbled and fractured. He saw himself reflected back from many different angles, all of them incomplete and imperfect, and all of them wearing the outfit he'd been so proud of before tonight. Tight black jeans with modest bondage straps, a black mesh vest. How predictable it looked.

He turned his head slowly and watched the different versions of himself follow. The line of his jaw drew his eye and he raised a hand to touch it. The skin of his neck was heated; stubble scratched his own palm.

"You feel invisible," said a voice behind him. "Even in this room of mirrors."

Ash jumped; a cold fear flooded him.

"Don't bother turning around," the voice said. It was soft and quite calm. "There's nothing of me to see."

Ash didn't need to turn around to know that this was true. He was standing in front of a wall of mirrors and they told him that there was nothing behind him but an empty room.

He unfroze his jaw to speak. "Am I on camera?" he asked. "Who are you?"

"I don't have a name," said the voice. "I don't need one."

Ash listened hard to the quality and tone of its words, trying to tell if they came from a hidden speaker. It was clear and very distinct, as if whoever was responsible was speaking directly into his ear.

"You can relax those shoulders—I'm not going to hurt you," the voice said, somewhat petulantly. "You looked so at ease before, quite oblivious to anything else. You should go back to that, it was much more enjoyable."

The urge to peek over his shoulder grew too strong. Ash twisted his head round as far as it would go and confirmed that there was indeed no one behind him. The knowledge filled him with exasperation, not fear, and he began searching the mirrors circling him. There had to be some explanation, he thought. A hidden person crouched in a corner seemed unlikely since he'd already explored the room. But microphones and speakers were much easier to hide.

"You're wasting my time *and* your own," said the voice. "You'll be done here much faster if you just get on with it."

Ash paused, looking up as the voice spoke and trying to fix the direction from which it came. "Get on with what?"

The Voice drew in a haughty, but invisible, breath. "This is the New Admissions Room," it said. "You were sent here, weren't you?"

Ash walked slowly towards it—the voice seemed to be located high up on the back wall, almost at the ceiling. He stood gazing up at the spot but without a ladder he wouldn't be able to get close enough to find the speaker.

"No one sent me here," he said. "What are you talking about?"

"Oh, *pardon me*," the Voice said. Ash imagined its owner with a curled lip. "'No one sent me here', *really*. As if you found this place all on your own."

"But I did," Ash insisted. "I was looking for—"

"And nothing," the Voice interrupted. "This is just stalling, a complete waste of time. Have you changed your mind? Is that it?"

"Changed my mind?" Ash's confusion was growing by the minute. And then he realised that he'd stopped searching for something to explain the Voice and had started arguing with it instead. "I don't understand. What am I supposed to be doing?"

"But surely it's obvious," the Voice said, this time not unkindly. "You're feeling a little frustrated, wanting to be accepted? Am I right?"

Ash paused, unwilling to respond even though he knew his silence was damning.

"Of course I am," the Voice continued, "because that's why you're here. So please, by all means"—there was a dramatic and deliberate pause, as if the Voice had gestured broadly—"be my guest."

Ash looked wildly into the mirrors in front of him but they only showed him his own shocked expression. *Be my guest?* he thought. *To do what?*

"Come, come," the Voice encouraged. "You're not invisible to me. Show me what you've got."

"This has to be a joke—" Ash began, but something touched his collarbone and made him start. He looked down: it was his own hand. In the mirror, he watched it glide across his sternum. "What the *actual fuck?*"

"That's it," the Voice said. It had changed its tone: instead of bossy and self-important, it became smooth, low, and coaxing. "Don't overthink—just lean into it."

Ash's hand slid across his chest, thumbing the ridge of his collarbone. Skin met his palm at the dip of his vest; goosebumps prickled his skin. He watched his hand move with astonishment. It felt as if someone else was touching him, a sensation both disturbing and pleasurable.

"Now you're getting the idea," the Voice purred. "Doesn't that feel good?"

Ash felt his head nodding in agreement. Pleasure spiked his blood; his nipples had peaked with arousal. His hand slipped underneath his vest to rub them. He let out a shocked gasp when his fingers pinched hard. "What is this?" he asked. "How are you doing this?"

"*I'm* not doing anything *you* don't want me to," the Voice said. "You want to join in, don't you? Become part of the group downstairs? They all had to come through me, you know."

The controlling power receded a little; Ash felt it lift and suddenly his hand was his own again. He lifted it to his face and flexed it in awe. The Voice behind him was silent, waiting.

"Yeah," Ash said with a swallow. "I do want to. I want to join in."

"I thought so," the Voice said.

The strange force took hold of Ash once more and this time it was stronger. His fingers moved with more certainty and the pleasure they caused seemed like the work of a hundred more.

"Am I on camera?" he asked again. He was staring at the picture he made in the mirror: vest pulled down to expose a single hard nipple, a flushed face with a half-open mouth. The outline of his erection was visible through his jeans. "You didn't answer before."

"There are no cameras," the Voice said. "No one else can see you, and no record of this will be kept."

There was a pause. When it spoke again, the sound was lower, a half-whisper.

"Concentrate on the mirror, on my Voice," it said. "Make

room inside yourself to receive what it is that you desire."

Ash's eyes fluttered closed. The hand at his hip was smoothing across the front of his jeans, its palm open and teasing. He forced them open and made himself watch. His own reflection confronted him: he looked good, he thought. Definitely worth a fuck.

"Yes," the Voice whispered. The angle of sound seemed to have changed—if it had been a person, it would've been standing right behind him. "They're going to like you *very much* downstairs."

Ash gasped, massaging himself through warm, rough denim. Watching himself was strange. He believed his movements to be his own, or at least he believed he could stop them if he wanted. But at the same time, they seemed to come from elsewhere. Was it the Voice or was it something else entirely?

"Don't you feel better?" the Voice said. "Just give in—make a space for me inside you."

Ash could almost imagine the Voice's breath tickling his ear. He'd started to attach images to it, as well: fleeting impressions of dark, trailing hair and calm, pale-eyed arrogance. He remembered the sensation of cold, cold liquid flowing down his throat. His mouth watered and a burst of fire flashed through his veins.

"Why don't you take yourself in hand?" suggested the Voice.

Ash unbuckled and, slipping a hand inside of his jeans, took hold of his cock. He was hot and hard; he could feel the weight of himself cushioned in his palm. But he could also feel the soft teasing squeeze of a stranger's fingers. Each sensation was distinct from the other, bizarre and incredible, and he let out a held-onto moan.

Surprisingly, so did the Voice. "You see?" it gasped. "*So good.*"

Ash's hand started to move in long, voluptuous strokes. It felt unreal: it was his hand and it wasn't, both at the same time.

"Perfect," the Voice groaned. "Don't stop—keep going."

Ash didn't need to be urged. He was electrified, caught in a feedback loop, manipulating himself with a firm, delicious touch.

"Show me," said the Voice. "Don't hide from the mirror. Show us both."

Ash's throat was tight with want. He freed his cock fully from his clothing and stood with his head tipped back, watching himself out of half-closed eyelids. What he saw was good, very good: dark vest and dark jeans framing his glossy, swollen hardness. His hand moved again, caressing, further spreading his leaking wetness along its length.

The Voice spoke again, half-breathless. "Taste it," it said. "Bring your finger to your mouth and—"

Before it could finish, Ash brought his hand up and sucked lasciviously, watching his cheeks hollow in the mirror.

The Voice moaned. Ash felt it rumble through him; the sound seemed to echo inside his head.

He felt powerful. Everything had changed and he seemed able to anticipate what the Voice wanted. Its instructions chimed with his inner desires and he was no longer surprised by the things it said.

"Do you like how you taste?" the Voice was saying, from a place which was somehow both inside and outside of him at the same time. "I do—warm, earthy, bitter. Rich and uniquely human. Like blood."

Ash didn't bother responding. The Voice already knew the answer; it could see it in his mind. He concentrated instead on pumping himself hard and fast, staring himself down in the mirror. The dust on its surface shimmered dully, as if the specks resting there had been subtly rearranged. In them, it was easy to read a sweep of long hair across his cheek, a pale unearthly hand in place of his own. And, if he looked carefully at his reflection, he could discern the faint, overlain shadow which had fallen across him.

"Make us come," the Voice whispered hoarsely. "Make us both come."

Ash took a step forward and, bracing himself on the grimy frame, obeyed. He felt something unusual: a rushing, vibrating burst of energy that surged through him. It seemed to go on and on, and with it he came hard across the glass. He groaned out his elation through gritted teeth and something else groaned along with him. Sharp fingernails dug into the meat of his hip and then, finally, let go.

When he opened his eyes again, his breathing was laboured and his shoulder hurt from holding himself up. He blinked a few times, feeling light-headed, and then met his own gaze in the glass.

There was only himself looking back.

He tucked away his softening cock and turned around. As before, there was nobody else there. But this time it was different—the Voice was silent. Not only silent, but gone.

Ash couldn't say how he knew it to be true. It just was. Maybe the air felt less dense or smelled less disturbed. Maybe the temperature was warmer or the light flatter. But all thoughts of hidden cameras and microphones had been driven from his mind. They couldn't explain what he'd encountered and he wasted little time in looking around before he left. He tried the door and, finding it unlocked, realised with a shiver that whilst inside he'd never once thought of leaving.

His journey back down the stairs to the fire exit was unremarkable. Nothing unusual happened and no lingering sense of the uncanny troubled his senses. But, once at the bottom, delayed disbelief accosted him. His knees buckled. He sat down heavily and waited for his heart to slow. He'd come to the club that night, innocent and hopeful, looking for a connection with someone, with Omar. What had he found instead?

But he had no time to dwell on the subject. Like a sudden mirage, the figure of Omar emerged from the smoking terrace. Ash stared, unwilling to believe he was real.

"Ash, at last!" Omar said. "I've been looking for you everywhere!"

His brown eyes were alight with warmth; he looked so very *good,* bright and mischievous and animated. He bounded forward with a hug; his hands lingered on Ash's arm, on his shoulder.

"I've got some people I'd like you to meet," he said. "We're going to the bar for a drink—want to join us?"

He seemed not to notice that Ash had collapsed at the bottom of a strange and dusty staircase, or that he looked exhausted and smelled of sex. There was such a strangeness to their meeting that Ash had to wonder what out of the ordinary thing Omar *would* have noticed. A tutu? A rabbit costume? He seemed so intent on fetching Ash to meet his friends that nothing else mattered.

"You want to join in, don't you?"

Ash's eyes widened. For a moment, he'd thought the Voice had come back but it was only an echo of a memory.

And Omar... Omar was the result of a bargain kept.

Ash paused only long enough to blink. "Yes," he said. "I'd love to join you."

It was as if a key had turned in a lock. The rest of the night passed in a blur of new friends and new experiences, exactly as Ash had hoped during his lonely vigil at the bar. In a quiet moment, he tried to ask Omar if he knew of a room upstairs filled with mirrors. But he was met with a blank look and quickly changed the subject.

That was when he decided that he had to speak to the barman again. The night had turned and the crush at the bar had quietened down. When Omar suggested a final round of drinks, Ash jumped at the chance.

"It's my turn," he said, waving down any opposition. "I'll get them in."

There was an odd feeling in his stomach as he waited. He hoped that another member of staff wouldn't get to him before the barman, but he didn't need to worry. The barman saw him and smiled.

"Come for another beer?"

"Yes," Ash said. "But first I wanted to ask you a question."

"Oh, yes, of course you do."

The barman leaned across the bar so that his face drew close to Ash's. His unusually pale irises were completely uniform in colour, but what that colour was Ash couldn't say.

"I can only tell you this," he said. "Everyone passes through the mirror room once—it's the price of admission."

Ash didn't respond. He didn't know how to. He just let his mouth fall open and it stayed that way.

"Six beers, is it?" the barman asked. "One each for you and your new friends?"

Ash swallowed and tried to pull himself together. "Six. Yes, that's right," he said. Had the barman been watching them or did he possess other means of knowing?

The barman ducked and grabbed them from a fridge underneath the counter. Ash could hear the bottles clinking and the caps being shucked off. Little else entered his mind. There was just the barman's curious presence and his pale, pale eyes.

"By tomorrow you'll have forgotten everything," the barman said in a consoling tone.

Ash felt like an upset child being soothed by a wise, patient grandparent: *everything will feel better in the morning*. It was too much. He threw the barman a desperate, confused look.

"But—"

"But you'll still have your friends." the barman said as he handed the beers over. "It's a fair exchange, don't you think?"

Was it fair? Ash didn't know. Dumbly, he reached for his wallet.

The barman stopped him. "It's on the house," he said, with a brilliant smile. "It's the least we can do for a new customer."

Ash met his eyes and realised it was useless to argue. "Was it you?" he asked, after a small pause.

But the barman just continued to smile. "Go enjoy your beer," he said. "Warm, earthy, and bitter. Just how we like it." And then he turned and was gone.

Ash frowned to himself. That didn't make sense, he thought. The beer in his hand was cold. Not *warm*.

He pushed back through the crowd, heading for the table where his friends were waiting. *His new friends.* Was it a fair exchange? he wondered. It didn't feel fair to have his memories taken from him—and the further he got from the pale-eyed barman, the more fiercely he wanted to fight for them.

He *would* remember, he told himself. It was the kind of thing which must surely be hard to forget. How could he not remember that eerie room? And the sound of the Voice mesmeric in his ear? The hand which was not his hand; the uncanny intimacy of a shadow in the mir—

A woman bumped his elbow, causing him to spill some beer. She was effusively apologetic, even offering to replace them. Ash smiled and told her not to worry—it was only a drop, no one would miss it, no harm done. She watched him as he walked away; her interest was open and inviting and it followed him through the crowd. He noticed a guy a few paces away checking him out too. Ash arrived back at his friend's table with a good and generous mood fizzing inside him.

He took his seat next to Omar, aware of something niggling the back of his mind. Something warm, almost nostalgic. He felt as if he'd been thinking of something which had happened long ago, but which had now slipped his thoughts.

Oh well, he thought, as Omar's hand settled onto the curve of his ass. Never mind. He had far more interesting things to attend to here. If it was that important, it would come back to him.

Wouldn't it?

6

Meeting Isaac

Hanging over the fireplace was a mirror. Though Isaac tried his hardest to avoid it, his reflection seemed to be inescapable, even when seated on the sofa. It was his own face which drew him in and it looked pinched and much too pale. His hair, too, was all wrong. Isaac fretted over it, moving it this way and that, but it made no difference at all. He'd styled it with such confidence that morning, in preparation for his appointment with Luis. Now, in the light of Luis's living room, it just seemed flat and colourless.

At the back of his mind, a small voice spoke up. It reminded him that when he was nervous he was prone to seeing himself in a negative light. The thought provided some comfort—but then he noticed the anxious expression of his eyes and the troubled line of his mouth. Those parts were real and they weren't very sexy. Daksh would take one look at him and lose interest.

It's not my hair that's the problem, Isaac thought. It's all this other stuff, all written across my face as plain as day.

With difficulty, he pulled his gaze back down to the floor—he didn't need to look at the mirror any more. He was still studying the muted patterns of the rug beneath his feet when Luis breezed in with his laptop.

"Ready?" he asked, all but clapping his hands together with enthusiasm. A woody, citrussy scent lagged behind him, a remnant of a recent shower.

"No," Isaac said. His palms had started to sweat; he wiped them on his jeans.

Luis, he noticed, was barefoot and, by most people's standards, only half-dressed. He wore a clingy pair of jogging bottoms and very little else. Unlike Isaac, he was never worried about what he looked like. It was a very attractive quality, Isaac realised. It was no wonder that Luis was so in demand.

"Do I look okay to you?" Isaac asked. "Do I look, well, *normal?*"

The desperation in his voice made Luis pause. He rarely, if ever, gave empty reassurances, but this time he stood back and appraised Isaac as carefully as one of his own paintings.

"You don't look any different to usual," Luis said, after a moment. "And you know I think you're as cute as hell." He tipped his head to one side, frowning. "Bit pale maybe. But honestly, even that's appealing on you."

"Are you sure?" Isaac said. "I just— I don't know, I caught sight of myself in that mirror and—"

"I'm sure," Luis said firmly. "And remember that Daksh already knows what you look like. So there's no need to take your trolley down the 'but what if he doesn't fancy me?' aisle of the worry supermarket."

"But that was just a photo—a good one," Isaac protested. "The reality won't match up to it, especially on a webcam. Everyone looks bad on those."

Luis grinned, mostly to himself, and settled onto the sofa close to Isaac. "You're forgetting that I'm a professional—I have a *very good webcam*."

A snort of nervous laughter erupted from Isaac. Self-conscious, he covered his mouth with his hand, and then felt Luis's fingers wrap around his wrist, warm and intimately steadying. A sigh built inside him; he let it out and allowed his shoulders to drop.

"These are completely normal nerves, you know," Luis said. "But is there anything else going on? It's easy to postpone if you're not having a good day. I can message Daksh now, it's not a big deal—"

"No," Isaac said, interrupting. "Don't. I just need to push through. If I stop and think about it too much, I won't be able to do this at all. Maybe never."

Luis's face grew more concerned. "Yes, but remember how we talked about baby steps? It's only a call, it doesn't mean anything. If you push yourself too hard, you'll forget to have any fun." His eyes flashed with impish glee and he nudged Isaac in the ribs. "After all, isn't that the whole point?"

Isaac frowned and hunkered down in on himself. "If I don't push myself then the bad stuff wins and I won't get any fun at all."

Luis leaned closer, kind and smiling and smelling of bergamot. "You've come a long way since I first met you," he said. "Don't forget that."

His brown eyes were bright and his tanned skin was beautifully clear. He seemed so clean and healthy, in both body and mind—so at ease with himself and the world. Isaac would've given anything to feel the same way.

"I think you can take your foot off the pedal a little," Luis said.

"Try to relax." He released Isaac's wrist and rubbed small circles across his back instead.

Isaac let the touch silently nourish him. Even though he'd only known Luis a few short weeks, he trusted him more than he'd ever before trusted anyone.

During their first meeting, all they had done was talk. Maybe Luis had held his hand while Isaac had poured his heart out—he couldn't quite remember. At their second meeting, Isaac had freaked out and insisted all the lights be turned off before they'd got down to anything more serious. But slowly, Luis had coaxed and encouraged. And Isaac had, in Luis's words, "blossomed".

Looking back, Isaac could see the progress he'd made. But there still wasn't enough of it to erase the shame of his needing to try so hard in the first place.

As a boy, he'd always been shy. And his upbringing—boarding school, its bullies, his parents and their demands—had morphed it into something much worse. Until recently, no matter how much he'd craved touch, something dark and panicked had prevented him from seeking it.

But then he'd found Luis and, with his help, had started to work on his fears. They'd shrunk so much over the past couple of months that there was now room for other things—things which Isaac could take out and show to Luis so that they could be examined in more detail. Eventually, Isaac had realised that he wanted to be overwhelmed to the point of distraction; to be swept somewhere far beyond the reach of his anxiety. What he wanted was—shockingly—more than that which Luis could provide on his own.

Ever accommodating, Luis had found a possible solution in Daksh. Isaac was to meet him first, in case something between them didn't click. And then, if everyone was agreeable, Luis would arrange the rest.

It all sounded great; so easy. Luis had a way of making everything seem like that. But, for Isaac, it meant continuing to battle through his old, nagging anxieties.

He looked down at his fists. They were white with determination. Perseverance, Luis had told him during their first meeting. You can do anything if you don't give up on yourself.

Isaac screwed up all of his courage. "Okay, let's do it," he said. "Let's call Daksh."

Luis beamed. "Your wish, et cetera," he said. He reached for his laptop and opened it. "I'll be here the whole time to look after you, as well."

Isaac nodded. The beginnings of excitement fizzed in his belly, intoxicating and a little dangerous. He watched as Luis balanced the laptop on one knee. There was a pause, and some clicking, and then Isaac heard Daksh's voice greeting Luis. The tilt of the screen meant he was only a dark shape on an even darker background, but he sounded at ease, as if arranging a threesome was an everyday matter.

And it probably was, Isaac thought. Not everyone had his problems. In fact, most guys seemed to be the opposite. Daksh's Instagram had been full of the kinds of hot, shirtless thirst traps that Isaac couldn't ever imagine taking. Daksh was tall, but not too tall; lean, but muscular. His hair was effortlessly messy and his skin glowed in tones of burnished copper. With stubble, he looked raspily-gorgeous; without, he was sleekly chiselled. And his chest hair was dark and manicured—better even than Luis's...

"And here's Isaac," Luis was suddenly saying, from somewhere very close by.

Isaac blinked and the screen was plonked into his lap.

His first reaction was to give silent thanks for the sticky note covering the thumbnail of his own face. It was very thoughtful of Luis, particularly as it would've been a crime to find himself distracted from the sight of Daksh.

He was even more good-looking than Isaac remembered. Perhaps he'd neglected to study his actual features? He'd got rather caught up with that picture of him still damp from the shower, with the towel sort of clinging around his hips...

"Hi Isaac," Daksh said. He wore a grin, one edged with a worrying amount of uncertainty.

That was when Isaac realised that the time for saying hello was already long past. And that he'd missed the entire conversation between Daksh and Luis, and so had no idea what to say to continue it.

Just for something to do, he waved at the screen—and then immediately wished that he hadn't. He could tell from Daksh's confused expression that he was making himself look weird.

"Hi," he said. "Yeah, this is Isaac." His heart was sinking; everything was going wrong.

But then Daksh smiled again, this time as if he couldn't suppress it. Like he was actually glad to be talking to Isaac and didn't care who knew it.

God, look at him, Isaac thought helplessly. His smile was beautiful, perfect; wide and genuine. A trustworthy smile; a fuck-me-now sort of smile. And he had dimples, too—the handsome kind, rather than the cute kind.

It turned out to be catching, too. Once it had got hold of him, Isaac couldn't stop his own from spreading across his face. "Sorry," he said. "I'm just really nervous. But I don't think I am, now—not any more."

Incredibly, Daksh was still smiling, still looking at Isaac like he might want to eat him up. Like he wanted to reach through the screen and do unspeakably good things to him.

Like maybe he actually would?

"Nice to meet you, Isaac," he said—and it was obvious that he meant it.

* * *

Luis left them to it. Getting to know Daksh on his own would be good for Isaac. And it was easy enough for him to keep an eye on things from the kitchen—though so far Isaac seemed to be managing pretty well without help.

As he diced an onion for that night's ragu, a few phrases drifted in from the living room. He heard Daksh admitting that he hadn't "done this" before, then hastily clarifying that he'd "done *this*" but not in such a planned way. Isaac's answering silence was a little loud, so Luis crept over to the door to check on him. He was curled up like a cat, engrossed in the story Daksh was telling about an underwhelming spur-of-the-moment threesome. It could have been a dangerous thing to talk about—Isaac was highly sensitive to anything which reminded him of his lack of experience—but he seemed so taken with Daksh that, for the moment, he'd forgotten to feel inadequate.

Luis went back to the ragu, pleased with himself. It was going even better than he'd hoped.

He often cooked between appointments, though not usually during them. Most of Luis's clients preferred to know nothing at all about his personal life—they wanted to pretend, briefly, that he was reserved only for them. But Isaac wasn't like the rest of his clients and neither did he harbour any fantasies about the transactional nature of their arrangement. He knew things about Luis. For instance, he knew that the ragu was for his boyfriend, and that Luis was looking forward to spending a rare, uninterrupted evening with him.

Afraid that he might be the type to cling, Luis had told him early on about Jay and had been surprised by Isaac's reaction. He'd seemed rather relieved, even interested, to learn that Luis was in a stable, committed relationship—perhaps because that was what he wanted for himself one day. He'd been looking for a safe place to learn—about sex, affection, and the language of touch. And, perhaps unconsciously, in Luis he'd found not only a teacher but an odd sort of role model.

From the beginning, he'd been a total sweetheart. Luis had found his messages almost by chance while emptying an unused inbox. These days, he rarely checked the professional profiles that he still kept up—his reputation preceded him and most new clients were personal referrals. But he'd stumbled over Isaac's DMs and discovered them to be disconcertingly heartfelt. In them, Isaac had revealed his crippling shyness and how his shame at having no sexual experience at the age of twenty-five was inhibiting him from doing anything about it. His therapist had suggested finding someone trusted to help him remove some of the mystique and Isaac had hoped—in the most unbelievably respectful language—that as a professional Luis would be willing to assist.

The photo which he'd provided—a strict rule of Luis's and one which he now knew would have caused agonies for Isaac to arrange—had sealed the deal. Isaac was as cute as a button—there was simply no other way to describe him. And he'd looked as vulnerable as he'd sounded, with mournful hazel eyes and hair the colour of pale straw. Looking at his picture, Luis had realised how horribly attractive he would've been to the wrong sort of men. Taking him on as a client had felt almost like a moral duty.

But he'd never regretted it. A client who could list up front all the ways in which they were messed up was far easier to deal with than one who lacked the self-awareness to do so. Isaac was a breeze: he was polite, he understood boundaries, and was plenty of fun when properly encouraged. All he'd needed was a bit of tenderness and then he was happily spilling his deepest, darkest desires into Luis's sympathetic ear.

Soon, though, Isaac would outgrow him—Luis could feel it coming. But it was right that he should. Meeting Daksh would be the first definite step towards Isaac finding his own way in the big wide world of sex.

He knew Daksh through a friend, one who Luis particularly trusted and who held the sort of parties that required a well-vetted guest list. Daksh was a regular attendee and Luis had had ample opportunity to observe him there. He was exactly Isaac's type—tall, dark, and handsome—and nobody had a bad word to say about him. The next time they'd met, Luis had put the prospect to him. He had a client, he'd said—a fact which he'd emphasised—who wanted a threesome. He needed something from the encounter that another professional could not give. Somebody relaxed, open, and friendly; somebody there just to have fun. Was Daksh interested? And then he'd shown Daksh the photo of Isaac that they'd taken together for that exact purpose.

Daksh might've been a *little* surprised, and he might've had a *few* questions, but a date had been set for them all to FaceTime. Isaac, Luis had explained, would need a virtual meeting to begin with. "He might seem extremely nervous," Luis had warned him. "But don't worry—he knows exactly what he wants underneath."

Laughter burst into the kitchen from the living room, loud and obviously flirtatious. Things still seemed to be going well. Luis washed his hands in the sink and then made himself a cup of tea. The ragu was finished, but he would wait until he heard Isaac wrapping it up before he went back in to join him.

It didn't take long. "Done?" he asked, poking his head around the door. Isaac was closing the lid of the laptop, looking pink and shyly pleased. "How did it go?"

Isaac demurred a little. "Good, I think?" he said. "I like him. I think that, maybe, he might like me."

"And I think that could be a bit of an understatement," Luis said, smiling at his overly-serious expression. He took his usual place beside Isaac and slipped an arm around his waist. "Tell me everything. What did you think of Daksh?"

"I thought he was really friendly—and not at all intimidating? I felt like I trusted him straight away."

Luis nodded. "That's good. And what about our plans? Are they on?"

Isaac blushed. "Yeah, I think they might be." Then he paused.

"Go on," Luis prompted. He bent to nuzzle Isaac's neck; he smelled deliciously overheated. "I want to know all."

"He made a joke about it being an audition," Isaac said, biting his lip. "He said he was ready to take off his shirt if it was needed to win him the part."

Luis laughed. "Didn't I say you'd do great?" He rubbed Isaac's chest through his soft sweater and kissed him gently, as a sort of reward. "But you should've taken him up on it—make the most of your casting director powers while you can."

Isaac sighed against him; he was quietly thrumming with unspent energy. "You know I couldn't have done it without your help."

Luis dipped his head again, this time making for the creamy skin above Isaac's collarbone. It was crowned with a beautiful rising flush. "If you close your eyes and picture it, can you see him with us?"

Isaac nodded tightly. His eyes were closed and his breath was short.

"What can you see him doing?" Luis asked.

But Isaac didn't answer—he still needed some encouragement to speak his thoughts aloud.

Luis pushed a hand beneath Isaac's sweater and thumbed his nipples roughly; they were sensitive and doing so never failed to get a reaction. "What can you see him doing?" he asked again.

Isaac gasped loudly. "Fuck! I can see— He— He's naked, and—"

Luis dragged his tongue up to Isaac's jaw and whispered in his ear. "Would it help if I told you that he's got a really great dick? I've seen it myself—you're going to absolutely love it."

"Shit," Isaac said. His eyes were wide, his mouth open; he stared at Luis with a glazed expression. "Really? Oh god. I want to suck him. I want to feel him in my mouth while you fuck me."

Luis smiled—with Isaac, it really was worth putting the effort in. "Well done," he said. "Want to practice? I've got your favourite dildo ready."

Isaac nodded, a look of naked want on his face. "God, yes. Yes please?"

* * *

Before knocking, Daksh paused to look up at the front of the house. It was nice, smallish, Victorian; well cared for. The sort of place that either of his married sisters would've been happy to live. There was a little lawn behind the low wall bordering the street and a few bushy herbs in pots by the doorstep. Flowers bobbed in pretty planted tubs under the windows.

Daksh checked again to make sure that the address matched the one given to him. It did. And he found himself wondering what, exactly, he'd expected instead.

He knew Luis moderately well—enough to say hello to and more than enough to flirt with. But the knowledge Daksh had of him didn't run deep. When asked, his friends had all agreed that Luis was sound, cementing the impression Daksh had first formed of him. To begin with, the arrangement had sounded nice and uncomplicated: just two hot guys looking for a third to join them. Even the news that Isaac was a client of Luis's hadn't worried him—quite the opposite. It had made everything feel simpler, with less chance of jealous repercussions or mixed messages.

But meeting Isaac had shifted something in Daksh's mind. There had been the pleasant shock of seeing him live on camera, all golden in the afternoon sunlight. His awkwardness had made an endearing change from the men he usually hooked up with. And, even when Isaac had relaxed, something sweetly vulnerable had remained beneath his smile. The memory of him had lingered in Daksh's thoughts long afterwards until at last the penny had dropped. This was not going to be the afternoon of convenient, casual sex that he'd initially envisaged.

It mattered to Isaac and it had to be good. For everyone, but most of all for him.

When he knocked on the door, Luis was prompt in answering. Somehow the way he was dressed managed to suggest nudity more indecently than the real thing. A pair of loose cotton sweatpants clung to his hips and a thin, near-transparent white vest skated over his chest. His hair was tousled; his grin was dazzling. Taken all together, it was a disarming combination—one that, on anyone else, would've been too suspiciously casual to be believed. But Luis got away with it—just. Though, after a few brief moments of blinking at him in the sunlight, Daksh realised he still had doubts. Was he trustworthy? What was he really like, underneath?

"Welcome," Luis said easily. He stepped back and gestured for Daksh to follow him. "Come on in."

He led Daksh straight through to the living room where Isaac was perched stiffly on the edge of the sofa.

Daksh's greeting was instinctive and so was his smile—but he faltered when Isaac failed to respond. His hands remained clutching each other between his drawn-up knees. He looked to be suffering badly, frozen with an inward fear.

There was an uncomfortable pause, one which dragged; only Luis seemed unaffected. Daksh searched for a few reassuring words, anything to break the silence. But Luis beat him to it.

"Would you like a drink?" He threw an assessing glance at Isaac and then moved towards the door. "It's probably easier to show you what I have, if you want to come with me into the kitchen?"

Daksh followed him. Luis closed the door smartly behind them and went over to the fridge. He opened it and handed Daksh a beer.

"That's all I've got, sorry," he said in a hushed voice. "Look, please don't worry about Isaac. He's okay, really. He just needs to acclimatise a bit."

Daksh frowned, and then frowned some more at the beer. It was one he'd never heard of, with a fancy bottle and a brightly coloured label.

Luis shrugged. "They're my boyfriend's," he said. "I don't drink. He likes them but, as far as I know, they might be crap."

He had a bottle opener in his hand. Daksh took it from him and sighed.

"Thanks." He shucked off the lid and drank some without tasting it. There was a sinking feeling in the pit of his stomach. "Isaac— You said he'd be nervous but he seems, I don't know—" Daksh paused to collect his thoughts. "Look, are you sure he's really okay with this? Because I'm not sure he looks it."

"He's a little overwhelmed, yes," Luis said. "But I promise you he's more than okay. This is important to him. We'll just give him some space and he'll be fine. More than fine. You'll see."

"Right." Daksh took another swig, bigger than the first. Was that true? The only thing to do was wait and see. "Right. Okay."

"And while we're here," Luis said, "I need to be extremely clear about a few things. Firstly, I'm here for Isaac. If he wants to stop, everything stops. Okay? In that scenario, there would be nothing else going on between me and you."

Daksh nodded. "Yeah, okay. Understood."

"Good. And the next thing is something I tell all my clients, though I know you aren't one. But you need to know it because of Isaac."

Daksh nodded again, half-absent from the conversation. He was still wondering about Isaac.

Luis's handsome face hardened; he leaned closer and spoke

low and fast. "The money only buys my time and attention, it doesn't get me hard," he said in a rapid undertone. "I only fuck people I want to fuck, and I don't tell lies and I don't make shit up."

It was all so sudden. Daksh nearly staggered backwards into the kitchen table.

"I can't introduce someone into our arrangement who thinks there's anything shameful or false about it. It could cause Isaac a massive setback and I won't risk that. He's worked too hard."

Luis propped himself up against the kitchen sink and crossed his arms. He was studying Daksh so intently that Daksh wondered if he could read the number on the bank card he had stashed in his shirt pocket.

"I hope you're not offended," Luis said, in slightly softer tones. "I feel sure you're not that kind of guy or I wouldn't have asked you here. But I do need to be absolutely certain."

Daksh shook his head. He wasn't offended—a little shocked, perhaps. But he felt a lot more settled in his opinion of Luis.

"No, I'm definitely not that kind of guy," he said. "And, actually, I'm glad you're looking out for Isaac. I know I've only spoken to him once but I can tell he deserves people who care about him."

Luis's expression lightened; his posture changed and his fierceness receded as if he'd taken off a disguise. "Well, I guess that concludes the interview part of our afternoon," he said. "Shall we see if Isaac's ready for us?"

But he paused by the door. His gaze lingered on Daksh; it was still assessing but now in quite a different way. And his grin, when it came, was exhilaratingly suggestive.

"He's been looking forward to this so much, you know," he said. "He's hardly stopped talking about you."

Daksh felt his eyebrows climb skyward; he broke into a laugh. "Man, I hope I'm not going to disappoint."

Luis smiled back. "You don't need to worry about that," he said. "Really. Isaac knows exactly what he wants—all you need to do is go with it."

He pushed the door to the living room open and disappeared through it. Daksh trailed behind, wondering what was going to happen next. It had been a wild ride already, and no one had yet taken off a single piece of clothing.

Isaac was still on the sofa, still looking wrapped up in himself—but he was less pale and even gave Daksh an apologetic smile when Luis sat beside him. Daksh took some encouragement from that and sat next to him too, though he was careful not to crowd him.

Luis spoke first. "Daksh brought you some beer," he said to Isaac.

His arms were clasped loosely around Isaac's waist and his chin rested on his shoulder. He met Daksh's eyes.

Daksh obediently held out the bottle to Isaac. "I had a little," he said. "Hope you don't mind. I was, um, nervous too." From behind Isaac's ear, Luis winked approvingly.

Isaac blinked up at Daksh as if waking from a dream. He took hold of the bottle and then threw his head back to drink from it. Daksh watched his throat work and, when he was finished, watched him smear the wetness from his lips with the back of his hand. In the flesh, his beauty was more robust than it had appeared onscreen. There he'd appeared smaller and more fragile than he really was.

"It's not you," Isaac said to Daksh. "I mean, yeah, it sort of is, because you're so— And I'm so— But, what I mean is—"

His expression was unbearably solemn. And it was sadness

that seemed to wall him off from Daksh now, not anxiety. Without thinking, Daksh reached for his hand. It was cold and damp from the bottle.

"You don't need to explain," Daksh said. "I know why I'm here and I know why you're here, too. So—"

His eyes were drawn down to Luis's hands—they were resting on Isaac's hips, just below his waistband.

Daksh swallowed. "Can I kiss you?"

Surprise lit up Isaac's face and Daksh laughed before he could stop himself. At first, he feared he'd made an error but, after a moment, Isaac joined in.

"I didn't realise that was such an unexpected question," Daksh teased. Isaac's mouth was coloured a deep petal pink; it was soft and curved uncertainly into a smile. "Considering why I'm here, surely you can't think I don't want to kiss you?"

Luis leaned nearer and whispered something into Isaac's ear. Isaac gasped and began to laugh again. He shook his head; his eyes were wide and sparkling.

"What did he say?" Daksh asked him.

Isaac blushed and didn't answer. But Luis was grinning to himself. He ruffled Isaac's hair affectionately. "I said that nice as it is, it's not your mouth that he's here for."

Daksh paused and bit his lip. A glance at Isaac confirmed that Luis's statement was very likely true. "Well," he said, edging closer to Isaac. "Maybe you'd better tell me a bit more about that?"

Luis threw Daksh a look of encouragement. His hands were busy; one had slipped down to Isaac's thigh and the other was settled low on his stomach. Both of them moved in small, caressing circles. He dipped his head and mouthed softly at Isaac's neck.

Isaac made a small, shocked noise. His eyes fluttered closed and, as Daksh watched, a shiver passed through him, one that seemed to dance across Daksh's skin as well.

"I want—" Isaac started, and then stopped, breathless.

Daksh leaned in. His chest was tight, his lungs felt too full. "What do you want?" He laid his knuckle lightly against Isaac's hot cheek. "Whatever it is, I'm here to give it to you."

Isaac wet his lips. He stared up at Daksh, his eyes plaintively huge. "I want—" he said again, just as Luis's hands slid upwards under his sweater. Daksh saw the rough pinch of thumb and forefinger; Isaac arched, gasping, half into Daksh's lap.

The words burst loudly out of him. "I want Luis to fuck me while I suck on your cock." Then he paused and blinked and gave Daksh a shy smile. "But you can kiss me as well if you'd like."

Daksh's world reduced to a point. A wave of lust seemed to have engulfed him; he floundered in it, temporarily at a loss.

Isaac seemed to feel the same—but then he lunged, clumsily, at Daksh.

And Daksh, only a fraction of a second behind, grabbed Isaac's jaw and pulled him in for a kiss.

His mouth, though soft, was demanding; and the sudden heat of him, sprawled across Daksh's lap, was unexpected. Even after his outburst, Daksh had thought he would need more time, more patience. But Isaac had broken through his reticence: he was fully astride Daksh, moaning with abandon and grinding himself against Daksh's dick.

Daksh wrapped his arms tight around him, trying to assist. But it seemed to hinder rather than help, so he palmed the front of Isaac's jeans instead and let him thrust against the heel of his hand.

Luis cleared his throat meaningfully. Both of them turned and found him shirtless in the middle of the room. He pointed upstairs.

In a flash, Isaac scrambled free. Daksh hurried after him. At the top of the stairs, he found Isaac waiting for him. He snatched hold of Daksh's hand and pulled him into a bedroom.

Luis was the last inside. He slipped off his sweatpants—underneath, perhaps sensibly, he wore nothing at all. Daksh rushed to catch up, unbuttoning the shirt he'd ironed especially and chucking it over the back of a chair. His t-shirt followed; Isaac was watching from the bed, his eyes bright and full of wanting. He looked delectably dishevelled, with his hair ruffled from Daksh's fingers and a neck marked faintly in red by Luis's mouth. The sight caused Daksh to fumble the buttons of his fly. All he wanted was that sweet and dirty mouth on him, exactly as Isaac had described.

Then he felt Luis's hand on his shoulder. Daksh looked up and saw Isaac shuffle closer to the foot of the bed. As if obeying instructions, he kneeled up; Luis touched his knuckle to his chin, then cupped his jaw. Smoothly, his thumb slipped over Isaac's lips and pushed into his mouth.

Isaac sighed; he opened wide and sucked deep. He was flushed and his jeans were unfastened; Daksh stared as he reached inside to stroke himself.

"That's it," Luis said. "It's okay to be greedy. We'll both take care of you, don't worry."

Daksh's efforts to undress slowed to a halt. All that existed was the wet plushness of Isaac's mouth enveloping Luis's thumb and his own steady heartbeat. It took what felt like an age for him to understand that Luis was stalling until he had finished undressing.

Daksh hurried to comply. When he peeled down his underwear, all of Isaac's attention was upon him. His cock sprang free; Isaac's mouth fell open and his eyes grew wide. Luis pulled his thumb away and turned instead to Daksh, encircling his fingers gently around his dick.

A groan built in Daksh's chest; Luis's touch was light but he could feel the wetness where Isaac's mouth had been.

Luis smiled and tilted Daksh's head towards his own; his kiss was fervent, passionate, practised. Something hot and hard bumped against Daksh's hip. Luis shifted his weight, and then he wrapped them both in his grip; working them slowly, steadily, together.

Below them, Isaac made a small choked sound. It was obvious what was coming next, and Daksh would have liked to have watched. But Luis's strong fingers threaded through his hair and held him in place. Luis kissed Daksh deeper, wetter, hotter; and Daksh marvelled at his choreography and his care. Caught up in the moment, Isaac would never notice how neatly Luis had given him the space to build up his courage.

There was a pause, one where Daksh became lost in enjoyment. Then there came a warm, sudden exhale on his skin and a tongue slipped tentatively along his length. Another hand joined Luis's, one that touched and explored rather than stroked and squeezed. Wet heat enveloped him in bursts, flickering between him and Luis. Daksh moaned loudly. So did Luis, and with evident satisfaction. He briefly met Daksh's eye, wearing a look that said *I told you he'd be alright.*

But he didn't allow Daksh time to get distracted. He pulled Daksh back into a series of long, open-mouthed kisses, with his body pressed close and his unoccupied hand firm on the back of Daksh's neck. It was only when Luis permitted it that

Daksh was able to take in the view of Isaac kneeling sweetly between them.

He was lost in his endeavours. With a pang, Daksh observed the line of his tightly-shut lashes and the redness of his spit-smeared lips. His cock had been pulled free of his jeans; occasionally he reached down and stroked himself absently. It was only when Luis grazed his face with the tips of his fingers, that he awoke from his reverie and caught Daksh's eye.

Daksh sucked in a breath. He wanted to grab hold of his hair and thrust fully into his mouth; to watch Isaac struggle to swallow him down— And he was pretty sure that Isaac wanted that, too.

But Luis had other plans. At some unspoken signal, Isaac drew back to sit down again, still staring at Daksh. Something had changed; Isaac was wriggling out of his jeans and Luis was helping. A look from Luis directed Daksh to the far end of the bed. He sat by the pillows and waited while Luis stooped to kiss Isaac, whispering words of encouragement into his mouth. Daksh watched them: the pale sweep of Isaac's spine, his upturned face, Luis's caressing hand working between his legs.

Suddenly Isaac was on all fours, crawling up the bed towards Daksh. His lips were parted, still swollen from the effort of pleasuring them both at once. Daksh touched his face as Luis had done, and Isaac angled his head towards him with a sigh. It was easy to follow the pattern which Luis had laid out—he offered Isaac his thumb and Isaac engulfed it with a moan.

And then Daksh found himself talking. His voice sounded strange and rusty, and he realised he hadn't spoken once since arriving upstairs.

"Fuck, you look so good," he said. He ran the fingers of his other hand through Isaac's hair and held onto the base of his skull. Each strand sheened with gold; his lips felt like silk around his thumb. "Does Luis tell you that?"

Isaac nodded, bobbing his mouth up and down with growing eagerness. His eyes were fixed on Daksh's, patient but imploring. Behind him Luis had rolled on a condom; his fingers were slick with lube.

Daksh gripped hold of his cock. Instead of kneeling up to give it to Isaac, he curled two of his fingers and pushed those inside his mouth along with his thumb. Timing was everything, he realised. He had to take his cues from Luis, or risk ending Isaac's fun too soon.

Isaac was sucking hard on his fingers. He squeezed Daksh's wrist and made a happy sound when Daksh pulled affectionately at his hair. Then he groaned; Luis had dipped his head to begin licking him open.

"Wish I could see what Luis can see," Daksh told him. "Not that this view isn't pretty."

But Isaac couldn't reply. His mouth pulled away; he dug his knees into the bed and moaned helplessly. He cast a pleading look up at Daksh.

Daksh in turn glanced back at Luis. He'd risen from behind Isaac, though his hand was still busy between his wide-open thighs.

"You ready, Isaac?" Luis said. He snaked alongside Isaac to whisper into his ear. "Ready for us both?"

Isaac nodded. His colour was high and his stuttering breath kept pace with the movements of Luis's hand.

"Good boy," Luis said, kissing his shoulder.

He straightened up behind Isaac; Daksh mirrored him. His cock brushed Isaac's cheek.

"You want this?" he said, holding it out to Isaac like an offering.

Tension rippled along Isaac's spine; with a quiet groan, Luis slid slowly inside him.

"Please..." Isaac whispered in response. "Oh, please."

Almost shaking, Daksh guided Isaac's mouth onto him. Isaac moaned, deep in his throat, and wrapped his lips around the flushed head. The heat of him and his flickering tongue was agonising.

"Oh, fuck yes," Daksh gasped. "Your mouth. Fuck. So beautiful."

There was too much for him to take in: the rhythmic nudge of Luis's hips against Isaac's ass, the muffled sounds of Isaac's enjoyment. His mouth was a furnace of pleasure; wet, open, accommodating.

"Want me to fuck your mouth?" Daksh asked. "Or—"

He didn't get a chance to finish. Isaac found the right angle and took him all, deep into his throat.

Daksh was left gasping, incoherent. "Fucking hell, you gorgeous little—"

Isaac's face was beatific, serene. The bridge of his nose had warmed to a delicate pink, flecked here and there with soft freckles; the dark sand of his eyelashes fluttered prettily. He withdrew and smiled.

"Angel!" Daksh finished, somewhat incredulously. "You gorgeous, greedy, fucking—"

Luis was laughing quietly at him, smirking and proud. "I told you so," he mouthed. He was fucking Isaac slowly but steadily, holding his hips in place and watching his progress with a careful eye. Then he reached underneath Isaac for his cock, and raised a questioning eyebrow at Daksh.

Daksh knew what he was being asked. He glanced down again at Isaac, at his petal-soft lips and saliva-slick chin. It seemed so soon, like they'd only just begun, but also he knew that Luis was right. His thighs were trembling; he ached like he hadn't ached in years. And Isaac was there, waiting, ready.

"Want me to come?" he asked Isaac.

Isaac's head was cradled in Daksh's hands. He opened his eyes; they were glazed but bright. He swallowed Daksh down once more and then pulled back, nodding.

"Where do you want it?" Daksh asked. He was much closer than he'd realised—even asking made his heart race. "In your mouth? On your face?"

Isaac didn't need to answer—what he wanted, he took, and with considerable style. Daksh could hardly believe the difference after his shy beginning. There was almost nothing at all for him to do—Isaac was fast and precise, jerking Daksh's cock whilst keeping the head cushioned on the flat of his tongue. Daksh's orgasm burst upon him; Isaac squeezed his eyes shut and chased it with his tongue.

Come streaked his cheeks and chin; entranced, Daksh fed him anything he missed with his fingers. He was still watching him trying to swallow it all when, at the end of the bed, Luis's hips jolted in a sudden, climactic manner. He groaned to himself and stroked Isaac fast; Isaac still had his mouth on Daksh when he came.

After that, Daksh could take no more. He slipped down onto the bed and lay on his back, talking all the while under his breath.

"Fuck, that was so good. Gorgeous— You fucking angel. So fucking good."

Isaac was balanced above him on shaky arms—Daksh

couldn't stop touching the parts of him that he could reach; his back, shoulders, chest, arms. He collapsed half on top of Daksh, exhausted and burning hot, smelling sharply of pennies and salt.

Over his shoulder, Luis ducked discreetly out of sight—presumably to dump the condom—and then slipped back in behind Isaac. He kissed the top of his head; Isaac groaned softly and snuffled further into Daksh's armpit.

"Did that really just happen?" Daksh asked the ceiling. Every muscle in his body ached. Even his arms.

Luis propped himself up on his elbow and stroked Isaac's back like he was a cat. He smiled knowingly. "I told you so," he said once again.

Isaac cracked open an eye and peered back over his shoulder. "What did you tell him?"

Luis smoothed the hair back from Isaac's forehead. "That he didn't have to worry about disappointing you."

"Oh." Isaac blinked and turned to look at Daksh. His face was a picture: half-surprised, half-confused, mostly asleep.

Daksh shrugged. "Yeah, I was worried about that," he said. "Though I don't think anyone could be disappointed with what we just did. Do you?"

He looked to Isaac for confirmation but realised there was no point. His weight was heavy and unmoving; his shoulders heaved with deep, slow breaths.

Daksh glanced over at Luis.

"Yeah, he does that," Luis said. "He'll be wide awake in a few minutes, though, so if you want some rest, I'd get it now. He may very well want to go again and, in my opinion, he's earned it."

He shoved a pillow under his head and closed his eyes.

"Again?" Daksh echoed. "Is that even possible?"

"I do what I can to accommodate," Luis said. "Worst case scenario, there's a box of dildos in the corner. I'm sure we can keep him entertained."

Daksh's mind reeled; he had too much to think about to get any sleep.

"If he wants to— And if *I* can accommodate— Can I fuck him next time? Would he like that?" he whispered. "And, like, maybe ask him out for a drink? Would that be okay? I don't know what the rules are for a situation like this."

Luis smiled into his pillow. "Answering that is far beyond my hourly rate," he said. "But that doesn't mean I'm not pleased you asked."

Daksh nodded to himself. That was good enough for now.

He glanced again at Isaac's sleeping face. It was crumpled into his side, soft and frowning. What a surprise he'd been. Would he be surprised if Daksh asked him out? Would he say yes?

He closed his eyes and tried to rest. Isaac would wake soon. And Daksh wanted to be there for him, in whatever fashion he required, when he did.

7

Devotions

The training hall was warm but draughty. A sudden breeze gusted from the empty fireplace, ruffling Benjamin's hair. Candles guttered in their sconces and wild shadowed figures danced across the scrubbed stone walls. Benjamin shifted his weight from side to side and tried to concentrate on David and Xavier. Letting his mind wander was not going to help him learn, but his legs, folded underneath himself, were growing numb and his thoughts were becoming unruly.

Another gust of wind caught the candle flames and the wall writhed with strange shapes once again. They seemed to be twisting, undulating, glorying in pleasure—

Benjamin squeezed his eyes shut and took a deep, steadying breath. He was not there to glory in anything but service, he reminded himself. Like Xavier. He must watch Xavier and concentrate.

Composed again, he focused back on his friend. Like Benjamin, Xavier was new to the Brotherhood and its strictures. He was bent low over David's lap and his whole body was moving with his efforts. His mouth was wet and plump, his cheeks hollowed. A small, satisfied grunt escaped his throat as he swallowed David deeper.

"No, no!" cried the broad-shouldered acolyte in charge of the training hall. "Not like that!" He came rushing over to Xavier's side and kneeled with him on the floor by David's feet.

Xavier's movements faltered. He pulled his mouth away and wiped it, bracing himself for censure.

But the broad-shouldered acolyte was practised at instructing novices and much kinder in his actions than in his words. "Look," he said. "Like *this*."

He began by adjusting the placement of Xavier's hands, easing their eager grip so that they lay softly upon David's bronzed thighs.

David was an acolyte, too, a volunteer for the novices to acquire their skills upon. His swollen member bobbed placidly between the three of them, shiny with spit and ripe as a plum. Benjamin gazed upon it, resisting the urge to wet his lips. It had been David's casual disrobing which had caused him to miss the broad-shouldered acolyte's name and now he was too afraid to ask it, in case he had to explain why his attention had so impiously wandered.

With the acolyte's encouragement, Xavier allowed his palms to graze slowly over the ridge of muscle which crested David's thighs. The fingertips of one hand reached the seam of his hip and paused there, gently stroking. Left outside of their little group, Benjamin fell to watching with dreamy detachment: two pairs of hands, two bent heads, David's sprawled legs and languid torso. Together, their skin made patterns of bronze, gold, and silver. It was quite beautiful, and he hoped that he could do as well when his turn came.

A moment passed. David's thigh shifted and a tightening twitch rippled its skin. A shiver of anticipation passed over his face.

The broad-shouldered acolyte spoke again. "Do you see the difference?" he said to Xavier. "Appreciate what is under your palms—cherish and respect it. Remember this is not a tumble in the hay—you're here to worship and to do so humbly."

Eager to please, Xavier nodded. But the trace of a frown still troubled his freckled face.

The acolyte gave him a reassuring smile. "Don't worry," he said. "The distinction will become more clear to you with time."

He patted Xavier's back and turned to address the wider room, his voice rising.

"Some of you will discover that you're not suited to the life we live here," he said.

A dozen pairs of young heads looked up from their endeavours. All were dressed as Benjamin and Xavier, in simple short linen tunics that carried little adornment.

"There's no shame in learning that," the acolyte continued. "What we ask you to do is not easy."

The stillness in the room grew; a few of the acolytes turned to listen too. Something important was coming: a clue to achieving success, to joining the hallowed ranks of the acolytes. Benjamin strained with all his might to both receive and understand it.

"You must be in control of your body yet supple of mind and spirit," the broad-shouldered acolyte continued. "There is power to be found on your knees—appreciate it but do not wield it. You must be humble in your Devotions, pious with your hands and your lips. Observe."

He swiftly bent his head to David's patient member. With his tongue he cradled the swollen tip and reverently tasted the fluid that welled there. Benjamin gazed wide-eyed at his upturned face and soft sandy eyelashes. David hummed in wordless approval and lay a hand in his curly hair like a blessing. A holy hush descended, almost as if from Heaven itself.

Then the acolyte released him to speak again to his rapt audience. "*Devotions,*" he repeated. "The Fathers train rigorously but you must not push them and nor must you tease. Know what part you are to play, learn it, and do no more."

Though none of them had been at the monastery for more than a couple of weeks, some of the novices nodded in a superior manner, as if this was advice they were well acquainted with. Benjamin tried his best to feel disdainful about such posturing—but a doubt crept into his mind about himself and his fitness for the life of an acolyte, and he couldn't cast away the notion that these novices might be the fabled few who were born to a life of Devotion.

Perhaps they had been practising it unknowingly all this time, he thought. Perhaps they'd never had a tumble just for the fun of it. One of his cousins at his aunt's farm had said something similar once, way back—that some were drawn to common worship for its own sake, rather than in the service of their own pleasure. And that those who did were made that way by the Divinity for a life in the Brotherhood. Benjamin hadn't credited it with much truth, especially once he'd grown and had learned a thing or two. It had seemed to him that his pleasure and the Divinity's were one and the same, but now, in the dim, dusty quiet of the training hall, he was suddenly far less sure it was that simple.

His gaze drifted back to David's proud length, still glistening from the Devotions already lavished upon it. It was waiting for him. His turn would come soon. He must do his best and not think of his desire to feel it spill hotly over his tongue, nor of the urgency which lay between his own thighs. These were not things for a novice to enjoy, and neither were they an acolyte's to give.

The broad-shouldered acolyte moved away from their little group and went to speak to the silent room from its middle. "Now," he said, "continue, and try to put my words into practice. I want you to pay particular attention to each other's efforts—you will learn faster that way. Take it in turns, and, if your acolyte offers you guidance, *listen to it*."

David stirred and stretched; then he reached out one of his arms and gently gestured Benjamin towards him. His smile was tranquil and inviting.

Benjamin shuffled closer; Xavier took his place on the floor and settled down, ready to watch. As they passed each other, a brief glance passed between them. Xavier was flushed, bright-eyed; a small smile played around his reddened lips. The front of his tunic was distended with the strength of his arousal.

Relief flooded Benjamin. He was not alone with his struggles or with his desires. As the broad-shouldered acolyte had said, his task was not easy and nor was it supposed to be.

He felt David's hand on the back of his shoulder. With care, Benjamin bent his head and took the first sweet step of his training.

* * *

By the time Benjamin had finally learned the name of broad-shouldered acolyte, another week had passed. His name was Sol and he was the most senior of them all. He was popular with many and reminded Benjamin of a farmhand he'd once known briefly and well: rustically handsome, his figure was firm and full of strength, and his smile was as sunny as ripe corn. Amongst his other duties, he was charged with readying the novices for entry into the Brotherhood.

The road of their progression was long and testing and they were still only in the first stages. Amidst such trials, Sol's patient and sympathetic instruction was a blessing. Every day in the training hall he watched over the novices' efforts with a kindly eye, encouraging, praising, and correcting. And then, at the end of practice, he sent them back to their quarters with some smiling advice to help them pass the difficulties of the night.

For the process of training had begun to take its toll upon the novices. Each day their burdens grew heavier and more persistent. Flanked by acolytes and with passions inflamed, the novices would move in pairs back from the hall to their dormitory, ready for meals, prayers, and bathing. Every awkward step reminded Benjamin of his urges, of the fulsome weight of his desire. It was the first real test that the novices were faced with: extreme self-restraint was key to joining the Brotherhood and, for the novices at least, there was no relief to be had.

It had not been too troublesome at first. Cold showers, prayer, and a silent supper of bean stew had staved off the worst before it was time to retire. But, as the days passed, sleep became elusive and fraught with trouble. At night, Benjamin lay in his narrow bunk, afraid to turn over lest in his sleep the straw mattress became a substitute for a hand or a willing mouth. Dreams were treacherous, as were his fragmented memories of the training hall. The key to self-control lay within his own mind, or so said Sol, but it was difficult to put into practise any of the meditations he'd been taught when the dormitory, yawning darkly around him, was filled with the restless sounds of those similarly afflicted.

Was that a cut-off gasp? Had someone weakened? A bedstead squeaked; irresistibly, Benjamin pictured a joyful thrust, the relief of release. Day by day, the number of novices had dwindled as each learned what staying would cost them. Outside, it was a green and vibrant spring. No doubt it had received them happily back into its fecund lushness and they would not regret their choice.

Benjamin, however, was not ready to give up. He remembered too fondly his journey along the narrow flower-studded lanes to the monastery. At its gates, he'd rang the great bell and had waited on one knee for his pledge to be heard. It had been a momentous day, one long-awaited—just over two weeks ago, yet also a lifetime when measured by other means. He'd become a new person since then, one devoted to learning the craft of true worship.

It had been his eighteenth birthday when he'd decided that it was his fate to join the Brotherhood. A fair had been held at one of the neighbouring villages, and he and his brothers had been allowed to go alone, unaccompanied by his mother or older sister. There, Benjamin had encountered the Brotherhood for the first time. A small band of acolytes, dressed in the modest grey they wore in the lay world, had set up a stall selling honey and garden preserves. Despite their drab clothing, they had exuded an air of calm and wise prosperity.

Benjamin had never seen anyone look so peaceful or content. Passers-by kept stopping to converse with them and he'd moved closer to eavesdrop. There, he'd heard requests for advice and for prayers. One wanted to discuss treatments for ailments of the eye and one humbly requested prayers for a sick child. One old matriarch had spoken with them at length about her mulberry tree and had taken away a small vial for her trouble.

The acolytes had listened carefully to each and every request, and their responses had been grave and impeccably sincere. Benjamin had watched them for as long as he could unnoticed—he had not dared to speak. In any case, even if he had been bold enough to sidle up to their stall, he had no question to ask of them.

But one of the older acolytes had beckoned him over and, pressing a jar of honey into his hand, had said, "Child, when you are ready to seek answers, you are ready to receive them. Willingness is all there is to the art of learning. Until then, enjoy your youth and do not worry."

Benjamin had blushed all over and had stammered out his thanks. The acolyte had laughed with beautiful white teeth and then had sent him gently on his way.

In the weeks following, Benjamin had thought of him often—and rather profanely, too, since the acolyte had been made lean and strong by years of work, and had had kind, mischievous eyes only a shade darker than his rich brown skin. They were the sort of eyes that had made Benjamin feel things that he had not felt before, and it had seemed natural for him to revisit that feeling many times over by himself. He'd sensed, strangely, that the acolyte would not mind Benjamin pleasuring himself over his image. And also, that if he had wanted Benjamin to stop, that a mysterious sign or omen would arrive to communicate his wishes.

None appeared, and so Benjamin did not stop. Later, he found a friend, one who looked a little like the acolyte, and with him he'd learned much of worship with another. Other friends had followed him, and as the acolyte had advised, Benjamin had enjoyed his youth without worry. Instead, he discovered much about himself—behind hedgerows, beneath trees, in the shelter of barns—and all the while he felt that he'd been set upon a path that was his to follow. Something had lodged in the back of his mind, another strange certainty, and it told him that what he'd seen at the fair had been his own future. That one day he would wear a grey tunic and dispense wisdom and honey amongst those he was bound to as a Brother.

He'd waited almost three years for his chance to join. The Brotherhood only accepted novices on a single day each year, and even then only those in their twenty-first year could apply. The opportunity he'd been granted was singular, fleeting; he couldn't throw it away through carelessness or a lack of resolve.

On Matriculation Day, when he'd neared the monastery's gates, the lanes had been full of hopeful young men from the surrounding towns and villages. Some had been turned away immediately, and some with gentle regrets a day or two after that. Which criteria had been used was a mystery to Benjamin; it did not seem to be looks, or creed, or the position of their families.

But perhaps, he realised now, it was something else. A sort of ambition, and maybe not that of their own. Many families desired to have a Brother amongst their ranks because of the honour it brought—but that did not mean that their sons were suited to the life that the Brotherhood lived.

In the two weeks which had passed since then, that much had become clear. Several novices had left of their own accord, swapping the plain scratchy tunics of their rank back for their own handsome clothing. Benjamin had watched one or two go with a pang of regret—fine, sturdy lads, both of them had been, and in his old life he would have wanted to know them better.

But, at the same time, he'd known that it was the right thing. There was a difference to them; they had something he didn't and vice versa. They had chafed, almost immediately, at the many rules they were expected to follow and at the restrictions placed upon them: eyes down, be silent, move as one. Everything was communal; a pair of acolytes watched over them always, day and night. They would not have survived even a single day of training.

That had only begun in their second week at the monastery. First, they had learned about its workings, while being kept strictly sequestered from it: the kitchens, the gardens, the stables; the great library, the temple, and the many chapels the Fathers used for personal prayer and reflection.

The Fathers were a mystery to many in the lay world, and commanded great respect whenever they emerged from the candlelight of the monastery to walk amongst the townsfolk. It had been thrilling for Benjamin to hear them spoken of as men, and by those who knew them intimately. As novices, they were, of course, still too lowly and unskilled to be allowed the privilege of assisting them in matters of worship. It would be a long time before they would be permitted to even witness the Fathers at their Devotions, and until then could only learn from the acolytes whose role it was to serve them.

To Benjamin, the idea that he might one day be called upon to do the same was still a little frightening. The Fathers seemed distant and removed, and he knew they would not tolerate any mistakes. He found even lying alone in his bunk with the memories of that day's training to be a challenge, so what would become of him if the calm, understanding acolytes he practised upon were substituted for a Father dressed in stern and masculine black? They followed different rules of chastity and would not have to withhold their release from Benjamin's eager, waiting tongue—

But there Benjamin wrested control of himself and, with a whimper of frustration, placed his hands securely under his head.

How did the acolytes manage it? he wondered. It seemed that even the idea of assisting a Father with his worship was enough to tempt him to lapse.

But then, he reminded himself, the acolytes did not live a life as strict as his. On certain occasions, they were allowed to reach their natural peak. Sometimes, he believed, it was even a requirement. And the Fathers could exercise their discretion, too, within the confines of their private chapels. Though the Brotherhood demanded self-sacrifice, its creed was one of mercy and kindness.

He just had to be patient, he thought. And then one day his turn might, maybe, come.

* * *

It was not the next day that Benjamin's patience was rewarded—he knew he needed to wait much longer than that to find alleviation for his troubles. But something else, something just as profound, happened instead which caused him to take courage.

It occurred after training, once the novices had filed into the showers to cleanse and refresh themselves. Anything which could provoke, such as an inviting look or an immodest bearing, was frowned deeply upon, so Benjamin kept his eyes cast down. All around him tunics were being removed, revealing the evidence of his fellow novices' struggles. His own was thrust upwards, swollen and wanting and hard to ignore.

The first shock of cold water took his breath away, along with some of his desire. All the novices knew that it was better to get that part over with—though freezing, the water brought much-needed relief. They stood in lines, still avoiding the sight of each other, wet and shivering beneath it. Shoulders were hunched, fists were clenched, until, gradually, the cold conquered them.

Benjamin softened, his blood cooled; he shut his eyes and surrendered himself to the spray.

After a while, the temperature of the water rose—the sign for them to begin washing. Benjamin reached for the soap and made sure he was focused and brisk. A lingering touch, a careless thought, might be all that was required to bring him back to a stand.

Silence reigned; all was quiet. Then, partially masked by the sound of the showers, a disturbance rippled along the standing rows of novices.

"A Father," Benjamin heard someone whisper. And, very soon, no one needed to pass whispers along, for it was plain that a Father was amongst them. A heeled footstep confirmed it, one that fell sharp and ringing on the tiled floor. The novices' feet were naked, the acolytes wore only soft sandals. There was no one else it could've been.

Benjamin turned instinctively. A blurred figure in black could be glimpsed through the spray and, next, a soft murmuring voice was heard. It was smooth and low, too quiet to be distinct. Beside it flowed the respectful tones of Thomas, one of the acolytes on duty.

He seemed to be accompanying the Father on a tour of inspection. All the novices seemed to realise this wonderful fact at once—the knowledge jumped between them like lightning. Shoulders stiffened, postures were corrected. Benjamin caught the widened eyes of Xavier, standing next to him in line. His expression was one of terror, tinged with purest elation.

They all waited, tense with expectation. Benjamin focused on the floor between his bare feet.

"Jasper, this is Father Dominic," Thomas could be heard saying at the other end of the room. "No need to be shy. Please turn around so he can see you."

The room's silence was now weighty and full of excitement: all were straining to hear over the pummel of cascading water. But Jasper's response was inaudible, or perhaps the Father had not required him to speak. There followed a shuffle, and a slight change to the rhythm of falling water—Jasper had once again taken his place under the spray.

The set of echoing footsteps moved on. From the corner of his eye, Benjamin could just see Thomas and the mysterious Father moving slowly in step, with their heads bent together in conference. Like Thomas, the Father was dark-haired, but a well-trimmed beard sculpted his face.

Not everyone was graced with an interview, Benjamin noticed. Some the Father viewed from a wordless distance and then passed silently on. Less frequently, he stopped and asked a short question or two.

Benjamin swallowed; a knot had tightened in his throat. Both options were alarming. Speaking to the Father seemed an impossible task, but if he passed by without saying anything then Benjamin would worry that he'd somehow displeased.

They were drawing nearer and nearer, moving closer down

the line towards him. Benjamin soaped himself without thinking, his chest tightening with every in-breath. Visions of his recent training began to resurface. *No, no, no,* he thought vehemently. But it was no good. His ears rang with echoes: moans and sighs, praises and corrections, and the wet slick sounds which accompanied them. His lips remembered the fleeting brush of silk-soft skin, his palms and fingers itched to feel hard muscle beneath them. Water thundered in his ears; his skin felt too small to contain what rose within.

And, to his horror, he was indeed rising again. Despair took hold of him and, in the midst of it, he threw a desperate glance towards Father Dominic. He was half-turned away, engaged in discussion with Thomas. His hair, beard and brows were all as black as his suit, and he had warm, sunburned skin and hands which looked capable and strong.

Benjamin whipped his gaze back to the floor, ashamed at himself for staring at a Father. But the damage was done. He had seen, in that one short glance, what it must be like to serve him. The acolytes he practised with were kindly and passive, but *he* would be different. The surety of his guidance would be absolute; his fingers would be light yet firm under Benjamin's jaw, upon his cheek. He would expect much and would invite even more—*true* Devotions, *real* worship, not the pale imitation which Benjamin had so far practised. His member flexed with want—Benjamin could've moaned with shame at its impudence. Obviously, he was not ready to serve; was hardly even ready to learn. But all the same, his greatest worry was now that he would *not* be chosen; that Father Dominic would pass him by without a second glance.

Voices intruded into his turmoil—Thomas and Father Dominic had halted at his neighbour. He listened fearfully as

Xavier was introduced and asked to step out of the shower. Benjamin froze, trying to compose himself, and over the beating of his heart heard nothing else.

Then, suddenly, it happened.

"Benjamin," Thomas said brightly. "Father Dominic would like to speak with you."

It had only seemed a second ago that Thomas had been talking to Xavier. Surprised, Benjamin spun around and found his gaze colliding directly with that of the Father's.

Shocked at himself, he looked quickly away. The curriculum had not yet covered the proper etiquette but he knew immediately that it had been too forward of him. He was a brand-new novice, humble and unschooled, and it seemed wrong for him to know that the Father had eyes of a particularly intense blue. Or that he was smiling, very slightly, at Benjamin.

"Come forward, Benjamin," Thomas said. "The Father has come to see how you're all getting on."

Benjamin did as he was instructed. After the warmth of the water, the air felt distinctly cold. His nipples grew peaked as if in pleasure and his skin tingled with goosebumps. He kept his eyes down, which meant that he could not escape the truth of his situation: that his member was still aroused and was merrily rousing itself even further.

Beneath it, he could see the Father's shined shoes, incongruous on the wet tile. His suit was closely-fitted, his thighs strong. A shadow of what nestled between them was visible below the fastenings of dark cloth.

Benjamin wet his lips. The familiar taste of the training hall still crouched on the flat of his tongue and his thoughts, once again, darted somewhere beyond his reach. He wondered how many Devotions the Father had received; how many acolytes had served him. He even wondered which kind of acolyte pleased him best, a thought so audacious that it caused him to blush.

"How did you find your training today, Benjamin?" Father Dominic asked. His voice was soft, low in pitch, and it simmered with an undercurrent of humour.

Benjamin flushed a little deeper. If the Father was amused, it must be because he could see very well for himself how he'd found his training.

"I learned I have a lot to learn," he answered quietly. He raised his head a little and looked up at the Father from under his lashes. "And that I must ready myself to receive my learning before I can acquire it."

The Father's smile was fleeting and unexpectedly bright. "It's a long path, but the end of it is there, waiting for you," he agreed. "The only useful thing you can do is to keep asking if it's something you really want."

Benjamin lifted his head again and this time met the Father's gaze fully. There was a warmth there, and something surprising, something decidedly irreverent. Benjamin hadn't expected that. He nodded, a little awed. "It is, sir," he said. "I do. Or I believe so, anyway."

"Well then, if your answer is yes, willingness is all there is to it," the Father said. "Willingness and perseverance. When you are ready for your learning, you will receive more of it than you can imagine."

Benjamin nodded again, more readily this time. There was an effortless calm to the Father which cooled some of the heat of his doubts. His blushes faded, his spine straightened.

"All of us have been where you are now," the Father assured him. "Even myself—we do understand what it's like." Then he fell silent and stood back a little to study Benjamin. "Turn around?" he asked. "All the way, slowly."

Benjamin complied, too aware of the awkward bump and sway of his hardness against his hip. The blush returned; he felt exposed, as sensitive to the Father's scrutiny as if it were touch. His member shivered, drawing attention to his desperation to please the man in front of him.

The Father noticed. "Anxious to serve, are we Benjamin?" he said. His blue eyes twinkled; an easy smile graced his face. "Good, very good. Stay eager and you'll go far."

And then it was over. Benjamin blinked and the Father had gone, taking Thomas with him. They walked without stopping down the remaining line of novices, the Father broad, much broader than Sol; a strong dark shape leavened with humour and sparkling blue eyes.

Benjamin stared dumbly after him until he realised his impropriety. He forced his body back under the shower, plunging it beneath the cascade of water. It caressed, renewing the ache in his groin and coiling pleasure deep in his belly. Excitement spiralled within him; his hardness strained for release against his stomach.

But Benjamin cared little. He raised his face to the spray and felt the stirrings of something he'd found only once before, on a day a few years hence at a simple country fair.

He knew what name to give it now: Devotion.

His lips framed its syllables silently and he smiled to himself, clutching a new kind of joy to his heart. He was willing. He was ready to seek answers. He wanted to learn.

For if all the Fathers were like that, it would be nothing short of sublime.

8

Send Me One Back

I decided to write this last night after everyone had gone to bed. Elis had sneaked into my room so we could mess around in the dark. For the first time, he kissed me. In four days our holiday will be over, so I don't have long left. I have to get it all down while it's still happening; before I forget what it was like.

All of us—me, my mum and dad, and Elis and his family—are sharing a villa in Tenerife at a place called Costa Adeje. It's up in the mountains with a load of other villas built for tourists, completely swamping what must once have been a nice, normal village. There's nothing here but a distant view of the sea and a mini-supermarket that sells paprika-flavoured crisps, English bacon, and little brown bottles of cheap beer. There's one cafe, which opens and closes whenever it wants, and a tiny bar serving all-day breakfasts alongside pints of Stella and sangria.

The tourists all head down to the coast when they want nightlife. It's full of restaurants and hotels, clubs and bars; much more like the kind of holiday that Elis and I were expecting. After a day or two here, we tried to break away to find some people our own age. Any of those clubs would've done, but we soon found that it's too far and too steep to walk. There is a bus, which is always packed, and it stops running at six every evening. Neither of us is insured to drive the minivan Elis's dad has rented, so we're pretty much stuck. In the evenings, we have a choice of going to whichever restaurant our parents have decided on or staying here alone. And it's exactly the same story during the day, too.

Ceri, the eldest of Elis's younger sisters, was as bored as we were. At first, she stayed at the villa with us, instead of going on our parents' day trips. But after a couple of days spent lying around the pool, she changed her mind. Anything was better than nothing, she said. Apparently, we're even more boring than driving for hours in the boiling hot sun to visit banana plantations. After that, we've had the place to ourselves most days.

We stay at the villa whenever we can. There's a pool so we can sunbathe and swim. There's plenty to eat and no one to bother us. For entertainment, we have each other.

A long time ago, when we were both little, Elis and his family used to live in the same village as us. His mum was friends with mine, and his dad and my dad worked at the same office. Their house was only a couple of streets away and we were always doing stuff together. But when we were about eleven, they moved to Australia. I don't remember much about it. I know there was a barbecue, which must have been their farewell party, but none of us kids really talked about it. We just carried on as usual until one day they were leaving. Elis's little sisters were too small to know anything was happening—now they're eleven and fourteen and don't remember me or my parents or the village.

When Elis first told us he was moving, we were all so impressed. We were sad as well, I think, underneath. But mainly impressed. Standing in the wet playground at break time, surrounded by mist and all that grey Welsh stone, I suppose Brisbane sounded glamorous. We pictured beaches and palm trees, endless summers, massive houses with swimming pools—nothing like life in Penybryn. He told us he was going to learn how to surf.

He didn't, though. I think he was annoyed that I remembered he'd said that. It spoiled the picture he was trying to project: cool, worldly, popular. Someone different, not a boy who'd grown up in rural Caerphilly. His accent is now an Australian one, he has a tan. (Mind you, so do I after more than a week of Tenerife—it's not that hard once you get some sun.) He obviously thought I'd be as impressed by him as I had been eight years ago.

I just thought it was funny. Elis was so caught up in appearances—the first thing he did when he arrived was complain that the villa's pool was smaller than the one they had at home. And, after he'd said it, he looked around to make sure I'd heard. It was comical, *so* clumsy. Later, he tried to tell me about this girl he'd been seeing—except it turned out that they weren't really seeing each other, or at least not yet. She was a friend of someone at uni, he saw her around a lot, they'd messaged a few times. She'd sent him a couple of pictures but it wasn't anything major, nothing she wouldn't be okay posting on her Instagram. He showed me one of her in a bikini, trying to brag about it, like this girl was proof of something. That he'd, I don't know, succeeded somehow.

He was desperate for her attention—it was never enough. And, a couple of days in, I realised it wasn't just hers he wanted, it was mine as well. He needed an audience to witness what little attention she did give him.

Because it wasn't that much, to be honest. I don't think she was that into him.

He spent ages posing for photos to send her—by the pool, in the pool, on the sunbed. He got as near as he dared to an actual dick pic, which is to say not that close at all. His pictures were more coy than that. He'd dip himself in the pool, to make sure his shorts were clinging just right, and then spend ages looking for artful angles. The sort where his dick casually made a guest appearance, as if that was going to clinch the deal. He narrated the whole thing for me, as well—showed me his photos, got me to help him choose which ones to use. It was hard to avoid getting involved as he was always on the sunbed right next to me. There was even what you might call some "massaging of the facts", though I didn't help out with that part. He did catch my eye, though, like we were sharing a secret joke.

This girl—Grace—usually replied back but never with the sort of selfies he was hoping for. I know he was frustrated. She could probably tell that none of it was really about her. He just wanted to prove something, to be admired.

I'm not sure he's all that different now, to be honest. Maybe he's a little more grown up. I don't know. Does that make me a mug?

I think, when he was doing all this, he thought I was inexperienced or something. I am much quieter than he is, less full of bravado. I don't particularly care what anyone thinks of me and I definitely didn't give a damn about his opinion—as if I was going to go around bragging about *my* conquests, especially to him. When he finally got around to asking me about the girls back home, I decided to cut him off before he got started.

I could see what was coming—banter, story swapping, "all lads together" stuff. I don't like it, it's not me.

So I told him straight out that I'm bisexual. I didn't know what to expect back from him but somehow it seemed to win me a few points. At the time, I thought that maybe, to him, being bisexual was as exotic as moving to Australia had seemed when we were eleven. For good measure, I made sure he knew that I didn't live in Caerphilly any more, that I'd moved to Bristol for uni. I told him what a great scene there was there, how I shared a house with a load of friends, that we'd all shagged each other at least once.

He changed towards me after he'd heard that. Not in a bad way—he just saw me in a new light, I suppose. And I noticed that he started to turn to me for attention, once Grace was out of the picture.

It was weird, at first. I have no idea if he even knew he was doing it. Possibly not, I'm still unclear about much of what goes on in his head. The photos took longer and longer to take, and he would leave his phone unchecked afterwards. He might have sent them to Grace, or he might not have done—I really don't know. But I do know that he stopped mentioning her name so much.

And then came other things, too. Instead of coming down from his room ready to swim and sunbathe, he would put on shorts and a t-shirt and then undress by the pool, while we talked whatever shit we were talking about that day. He spent ages diving into the water and getting out again, diving in and getting out. Every time, he would stand dripping between our sunbeds with his back to me, leisurely drying himself off. It was obvious he wanted me to look at him but I tried not to give in. Whatever he was playing at, I wasn't really into it.

I did find it difficult not to, though—there's no getting away from it, he's nice-looking. I know I've been quite harsh on him so far, but if he'd sent me the photos he took for Grace, I would've asked him for a dick pic and then followed it up with one of my own.

It wasn't until I caught him looking at me that I properly understood what was going on. I'd been asleep, I think—I used to sleep a lot during those first few days. It was so hot, and there was nothing to do. Everything was quiet. Our families had gone out and we weren't expecting them back until later that afternoon. I woke up really suddenly, though not in a panic, not like when my alarm goes off on a Monday morning. I just remember opening my eyes and being immediately, intensely aware of all that sky and hot concrete around me. It was peaceful and good—my body felt rested and loose, like I was floating in the pool.

I turned my head towards his sunbed—I'm not sure why. Did I know that he was looking at me? I caught his eye and he smiled back. He looked a bit smug, like he often did, but also sort of excited. I didn't move. I gave him time to really take in his fill—all the way down to my dick and back up again. His hand was resting on his stomach, and it made me think of his own curled up snug in his swimming trunks, of him touching himself while he watched me sleep.

The next time he went into the pool, I followed him. I wanted to see what would happen. I guessed he was looking for an excuse to touch me, so I gave him an opening by throwing a beach ball at his head. Childish, I know, but it worked. The beach ball battle turned into a fight over a lilo, which turned into a wrestling match. We splashed and shrieked like lunatics, like kids, until I felt his hard dick against my thigh. We ended up in the shallow end rubbing ourselves off against each other—he had his hands on the wall behind him to steady himself. We kept our swimsuits on; afterwards, laughing, he peeled his back to show me how much he'd cum. I dared him to taste it and, without hesitating, he did. And then he said that maybe I should taste it too.

I didn't get chance, though, as our parents came back about five minutes after that. We heard them call out to us and had to rush to rinse ourselves off in the downstairs bathroom. There was a lot of noise—voices, hurrying footsteps, Elis's little sister Catrin singing something from the radio. We found ourselves in the midst of the daily scramble for showers—they'd booked a table at six, and Elis and I were to go too. I remember sharing a look with him when we realised there was no getting out of it.

That evening was a strange one. My mind was elsewhere and so was Elis's. He thought he was playing it cool, but he stared at me for most of the night. I don't think anyone else noticed, though.

All this happened within a few days of arriving, about halfway through the first week in. Looking back now, it seems like it took much longer. It seems like we've been here for months, and that we've still got months to go. I think it's because we're together so much, everything is out of context and difficult to measure. And the heat makes time feel slowed down. Four days left. I wonder—

He knocked on my door just then and interrupted me. It's late at night. I've been grabbing every moment I can to get this written down, on my phone, on my laptop. Anywhere. I don't want to forget anything, no matter how small.

We had to do it on the floor so we didn't make the bed squeak.

And, of course, we had to keep all the lights off. In my room it's different to what it was like by the pool. We have to whisper and I can only see his face when I'm up close to him. I sucked him and he sucked me, which I like because I can concentrate on what I'm doing to him and then on what he's doing to me. He's getting good at taking me now, and he cums so hard afterwards.

He's still smug, but now it's more like he's sharing his smugness with me, rather than trying to score points. He still likes to show off—how hard he is, how much of me he can swallow, how often he can cum—but I think that, this time, it might just be for me?

I don't know what he thinks about me, though, and I don't know what I think about him. Once he'd gone, I stayed on the floor, wondering if maybe I should be feeling something I wasn't feeling. Or perhaps it was the other way around. But then I realised that there's no time for anything like that. All we have are moments—moments of heat and secrecy. Breath on my belly, sweat on his thigh, the grip of his hand on my shoulder. When he cums, he groans and pulls his lips back over his teeth; he looks like he's in pain. Then he laughs, and kisses me, and I think about how many months four days can last for.

* * *

After that first time by the pool, I knew it was going to happen again. We didn't talk about it. It was just understood that it was what we were doing, and that we were going to do it every chance we had.

For days there was no one around but us, and nothing to do but get hard and cum, over and over and over. We had an incredible time. To begin with, he pretended to be asleep and lie baking in the sun with his dick tenting his shorts. He looked ridiculous. Or, at least, he did until I went over and pulled them down so I could suck him off. He was much more upfront after that. We liked to watch each other on our sunbeds as we stroked ourselves, him all stretched out so I could see every flex and quiver. I pulled his trick of pretending to be asleep and for the first time felt his mouth on me. I stayed still and let him do his best. When I was ready to cum he watched me, and then made himself cum as well.

Once, after I'd cooled off with another swim, I came back to find he'd put himself on display for me. His dick was arched against his belly almost ready to go off, so I challenged him to cum without touching himself. He didn't seem to understand what I was talking about and I realised I wanted to show him. It was risky. It was about three in the afternoon but our families were due back at four and what I needed was in my room. I offered to anyway.

I didn't know if he was going to agree to come up. Messing around by the side of the pool, under the heat of that sun, made everything between us unreal, somehow. There were the bright, hypnotic reflections of the water and the yellow liquidity of the light. The air was heavy, sultry. It was a different world, one easy to get lost in. Coming to my room might have been too much to ask of him.

I could have understood that, if so. I don't know what he thinks I'm like normally, but I've never been like this before—not with anyone. This is new to me, too.

Anyway, he did come up. I closed my door, took off my wet trunks and got straight into it—there wasn't any time to waste. Once I'd got my fingers fully inside me, my dick woke up and quickly got the idea—I've had a lot of practice at this. Elis sat on my bed and watched, interested at first, and then amazed when he realised I was going to cum just from that. After I'd finished, he asked if he could try, if I would show him what to do.

I think that was the only time he asked me anything like that. If there was something he wanted, usually he would just dive in clumsily on his own and let me correct him if he needed it.

I gave him the lube and showed him how to loosen himself up and then what to do with his fingers once he was comfortable. I didn't touch him myself; I just gave instructions and advice. Watching him was weird, like an out of body experience or something. I had to pay attention to his face, to his body language, to guess what he was feeling and thinking. I got a bit lost in it, in that fuzzy space between us. Imagining what his fingers were doing and how they felt was like being inside him and being him at the same time. When he came—all over my sheets, by the way, instead of on the towel I'd put down—I felt weirdly proud.

He was proud, too. I don't think he'd imagined he would like it, but he does. Just last night, when I was sucking him off, I touched him behind his balls and stroked his hole. He shot in my mouth with no warning—I almost choked but I didn't mind. I'm so greedy for him, it's like an obsession.

I wonder if he wants me to fuck him?

Our poolside fun, though, came to an abrupt end. Our parents—and, to a lesser extent, Catrin (Ceri didn't care either way)—were getting fed up with us staying at the villa all the time. It was a joint family holiday, they said, one which had been planned for ages and which was unlikely to ever be repeated. The first week had gone, they said, and we were going to spend the rest of it together. No arguments.

I could see that a proper row was brewing. Elis wanted to argue with them, but what could he really say? That the two of us were only interested in shagging each other senseless by the pool? So I intervened and agreed. For a moment he looked furious, but he must've caught on that I had a plan because he swallowed it and stayed quiet. When we were alone again, I pointed out to him that we had our own rooms. All we had to do was wait for the rest of the house to go to sleep, and then we were free to do whatever we wanted.

Never one to lose gracefully, he sighed in a put-upon way but said that he saw my logic. Getting away with things, he said, was always a lot easier when the people around you aren't looking for a reason to be mad.

So now we spend our days visiting markets and beaches on the other side of the island. Or volcanos and villages in the mountains. It's odd—the same heat is there, the same compulsion, creeping under our clothes and turning us to liquid. Sometimes I catch his eye when we're driving, or when we're sitting across from each other on a picnic bench, and I know he's thinking of it too. Of his hand on me, my mouth on him, our cum sticky across our skins. But we can't do anything about it, not until it gets dark.

There was one time, only a day ago, when we managed to escape into some sand dunes. The tide was out—we'd left our families camped beside the shore and had gone to explore. The dunes were huge and maze-like—I kissed him and pushed him back against one of them. Because of the sand blowing everywhere and the risk of being caught, we had to keep it in our swimsuits exactly as we'd done in the pool that first time. Afterwards, we waded into the sea and stood looking out, side-by-side.

I've caught up now with the story I'm telling—in four days it will be over. Neither of us will be here; we will both be somewhere else, emphatically apart. I can't wrap my head around the way time is passing. I know the days are counting down but the moments they're made of seem syrupy and slow—I can't think beyond them. Sometimes I wonder what difference it would make if we both were going home together, to the same country. The same continent, even. Would we carry on what we've started? Something makes me doubt it. Elis will quickly move on, I think. He'll find someone else's attention to crave and I guess I'll just go back to the life I had before.

It won't be too bad. But it won't be the same, either.

* * *

We had a fight last night.

Elis had just cum. With all the lights off it was dark, except for a silvery glow through the window—I guess from the moon. I lay down on the floor. The tiles were cold beneath the blanket I'd put down for us. Elis joined me. I could still taste him in my mouth.

Then, out of nowhere, he said: *Grace sent me a picture of her tits. I don't know why—I haven't spoken to her in ages. Want to see?*

I stared at him. He sounded indifferent, as if he didn't care about it either way.

No, I don't want to see, I told him. *She sent it to you, not me, you idiot. Don't go being like that.*

Alright, he said, all testy. *Calm down. Are you jealous or something?*

Though I was annoyed with him already, that was what really

caused the argument. I told him what a dickhead he was being and he said that I was being the dickhead, and then I was alone again. I slept badly, not because I missed him—he never slept in my bed or anything like that—but because I was still fuming. I'm under no illusions about him—I know he's immature and selfish and vain—but I was mad at him for spoiling the last of our holiday. And I knew that *he* knew that he'd fucked up, but he just couldn't own up to it, not even for the sake of our last couple of days.

We didn't speak to each other for all of today. Our parents took us to a water park and Elis spent the day being ostentatiously nice to Catrin, who he usually ignored. I talked as little as possible and, when we were all crammed into the minivan, I listened to music and looked out of the window. Me and Ceri were a right pair—Dad accused me of being in "one of my moods" but thankfully no one was listening.

But once everyone had gone to bed, Elis visited me exactly the same as usual—he left my room about an hour ago. I had gone to bed, sure I wouldn't be seeing him again, and had treated myself to some very vivid fantasies about making him beg for my dick and cumming on his face while he told me how sorry he was. I felt better after that, much less angry, so when he tapped on my door and asked to come in, I let him. His apology wasn't much, just *you're right, I am a dickhead,* but it was still gratifying. And then he was kissing me, and that was gratifying, too.

I almost got my fantasy, as well. I didn't wait to see what he wanted, apart from my forgiveness. I just made him strip and lie down on his front so I could rub between his arse cheeks and cum all over his back. That was another thing I found gratifying, especially as he seemed to enjoy it as much as I did.

Afterwards, I asked him about Grace. *What are you going to do?* I said. *Are you going to see her when you get home?*

He shrugged and turned over and told me he didn't know.

You can't ignore her, I told him. *You've been chasing her for weeks, you have to respond. Don't leave her hanging.*

But what am I supposed to say? he asked.

Don't say anything, I said. *Send her a photo.*

He was oddly quiet, so I tried to make a joke to lighten the mood.

What about that dick pic? I said. *Bet I could help you take a really good one.*

I reached over for him. He hadn't cum yet, but he wasn't as hard as he had been. I coaxed him back up to form—he has a great dick, have I mentioned that? It's no wonder he wants to show it off.

He closed his eyes and let me rub him off. I would've liked to feel him cum on me, too, but I didn't like to ask. He was tense and very still—unusual for him. I just let him do what he needed to do, and when he'd done it, I stayed quiet.

Eventually, he said: *I can't send her a dick pic—it's not right. I'm supposed to be thinking of her when I take it and I'm not. I'm not thinking of her at all.*

Both of us were silent after that.

We're leaving in two days.

* * *

I fucked him last night.

Elis was different again. Not tense like he'd been when we'd made up, but soft and sort of yielding. He'd given something up, I think, some kind of pretence. Last night, last chance, I guess. Real now or never stuff.

He made this sound when I was inside him, very soft and quiet, close to a groan. I can't describe it—it was almost longing. He really wanted it. I fucked him as hard as I dare, imagining that he was thinking the same thoughts I was, about fucking him so deep that something would remain. So that he could never go back on the time we'd spent together.

He was arching up to meet me, his arse smooth and round. Inside he was pure heat, slick from my fingers, tight around my dick. I ground into him, my mouth by his ear, and told him things.

I told him how he felt in my hand, how he tasted, what he looked like underneath me. Finally, I told him I would not forget. And then, before I came, I asked him not to either.

Don't forget, don't forget this, don't forget me.

I can hear myself saying that even here, on this airport bench, surrounded by suitcases and noise and aimless, rushing people.

I'm writing this on my phone and the goodbyes have already happened. Ours took place that night and the official ones took place this morning. Elis's flight has already left. He and his family had to be at the airport for six—our flight is much later, but we agreed to get up early to see them off. It was utter chaos—bags everywhere, everyone yawning, trying to eat breakfast and finish packing at the same time. Mum was cleaning, worrying over the leftover food in the fridge and making us eat stray yoghurts and bits of cheese. Elis and I had no time to say anything to each other and I don't know what else we could have said, anyway. Dad went to help Elis's dad load up the minivan. We waved; they waved back. And then he was gone and I had my packing to finish.

Before the taxi came for us, I went out to the pool. The water was so perfectly still, glowing with that fake aqua colour that pools always seem to have. It looked beautiful, I thought. The sunbeds were still there—now cushion-less, since Mum, worried about rain in a place which doesn't seem to have any, had brought them in. Otherwise, they were exactly as we had left them.

I took a photo and thought about sending it to Elis.

But he beat me to it—and it was a good thing that I'd had my phone on me. If I'd left it lying around, god knows what might have happened. I mean, anyone could have seen the picture he sent.

I knew his dick would look great in a photo. He'd done a really good job, too. He was always great at selfies—I suppose because he puts the effort in.

Don't forget, it was captioned. *And don't leave me hanging. Send me one back.*

Thank you so much for reading! I do hope you enjoyed this book and that you'll consider leaving a review on the site it was purchased from. It makes a big difference, especially to indie authors!

Thanks again, dear reader, and I hope to meet you again soon :)

The Book of Elis—coming summer 2022

Two childhood friends are reunited on a family vacation. Elis is self-obsessed, vain, and desperate for attention. Stuck in a Spanish villa alongside him, Ieuan, our diary-writing hero, is drawn into a surprisingly tender romance.

But once the holiday is over, Elis must go back to Brisbane and Ieuan to a rainy village north of Cardiff. Though they remain in touch, Ieuan's expectations of Elis are low. He is unreliable and immature—soon he'll tire of the novelty of their relationship and the distance keeping them apart.

Or so he thinks. Because Elis is full of surprises, and Ieuan has to decide how much of his heart he dares to trust him with.

- holiday romance
- childhood friends
- coming of age
- coming out
- long distance relationship
- secret diary
- setting: contemporary Tenerife, Wales, England, and Australia
- feel: angsty young men, plenty of feels and longing
- heat level: high

- length: 30,000 words
- stand-alone romance with a Happy For Now ending

Join my mailing list for updates on this and other forthcoming books!

Get a free story

Subscribe to my mailing list for news, updates, and promotions, and receive *A Very Personal Assistant,* a free m/m erotic short story, as a thank you! No strings attached :)

About *A Very Personal Assistant:*

Alistair's friend and flatmate Liam has just been mugged. Alistair, an unflappable but temporarily unemployed private personal assistant, steps in to… make things a whole lot better.

- hurt and comfort
- straight best friend
- flatmates
- contemporary London setting
- heat level: high
- length: 4,600 words
- stand-alone short with a Happy For Now ending

About the Author

Lou Skelton writes fun, filthy and feelsy gay romance stories from her home in south east London. She particularly enjoys subverting romantic tropes and heteronormative narratives, but she still loves a good, old-fashioned happy ending. She has several books in development and is currently working on her first series.

You can connect with me on:

- http://www.louskelton.com
- https://twitter.com/lou__skelton
- https://www.instagram.com/lou_skelton_writes
- https://www.goodreads.com/lou_skelton

Subscribe to my newsletter:

- https://www.louskelton.com/newsletter

www.ingramcontent.com/pod-product-compliance
Lightning Source LLC
LaVergne TN
LVHW091330150826
845673LV00006B/1818

* 9 7 8 1 7 3 9 7 8 6 1 1 3 *